LAST THINGS

D0277262

LAST THINGS

JENNY OFFILL

BLOOMSBURY

I would like to thank the following institutions for their support during the writing of this book: the Centrum Foundation, the Corporation of Yaddo, the Ragdale Foundation, and the Ucross Foundation. Many thanks as well to my family and to Ethan Nosowsky and Sally Wofford-Girand. And, finally, I am indebted to Doris Betts, Beth Meekins, Calvin Walden, and Marysue Rucci, who made all the difference in the beginning.

Portions of this book have appeared in different form in *Black Warrior Review*, *Story*, and *San Francisco Review of Books*

First published in Great Britain 1999
This paperback edition published 2000

Copyright © 1999 by Jenny Offill

The moral right of the author has been asserted

Bloomsbury Publishing Plc, 38 Soho Square, London, W1V 5DF

A CIP catalogue record for this book
is available from the British Library

ISBN 0 7475 4598 7

10 9 8 7 6 5 4 3 2 1

Typeset by Hewer Text Limited, Edinburgh
Printed in Great Britain by Clays Limited, St Ives plc

FOR MY GRANDPARENTS

Put your trust in the inexhaustible character of the murmur.

– André Breton

1

'Once,' my mother said, 'there was no true darkness. Even at night, the moon was as bright as the sun. The only difference was that the light was blue. You could see clearly for miles and miles and it was never cold. And this was called twilight.'

'Why twi?' I asked.

'Because it rhymes with sky,' my mother said. 'It's a code word for blue.' Code blue was what they said when someone died, I remembered, and this, too, had to do with the sky.

One day God called the bat to him and gave him a basket to carry to the moon. The basket was filled with darkness, but God didn't tell him what it was. Instead, he said, 'Take this to the moon. I'll explain everything when you return.' So the bat set off for the moon with the basket on his back. He flew toward the sky, but the moon saw him and hid behind a cloud. The bat grew tired and stopped for a rest. He put down the basket and went off to find something to eat. While he was gone, other animals came along. (Dogs and wolves mostly, also a badger with a broken paw.) These animals thought there might be food in the basket and pried the cover off, but inside there was only darkness, which they had never seen before. The dogs and wolves tried to pull it out and play with it, but it slipped away between their teeth and slithered off. Just then, the bat returned. He opened the basket and found it empty. The other animals disappeared into the night. The bat flew off to try to recapture the darkness. He could see it everywhere, but he couldn't fit it back inside his basket, no matter how he tried. And that is why the bat sleeps all day and flies all night. He's still trying to catch the dark.

'Which part of the story was the part about Africa?' I wanted to know. I had asked my mother to tell me about Africa and instead she had told me about the bat. 'It's all about Africa,' my mother said, frowning. 'Everything except the part about God.'

When my mother was very young, she lived in Tanzania and studied birds. It was there that she met my father. He had come to Africa to set up a fishery and she had taught him some Swahili and that was that. 'Before you were born, I met him,' my mother said. 'Before you were even a gleam in my eye.' This made her laugh. I laughed too. I had seen a picture of my parents in Africa, standing on the beach, holding a giant silver fish between them. When they lived in Tanzania, my mother said, village boys would wait near the trees at dusk and scoop bats out of the sky with nets.

In my notebook, I wrote:

ornithologist
Tanzania
fishery
Swahili
a bat is not a bird = *mammal*

My mother spelled out each word for me and later I added 'idealistic' to the list, which is what she said my father had been once. I kept the notebook because I thought that I might want to be a detective someday. I wrote down everything I heard, and when the pages started to fall out, I stuck them back inside with glue. I had an idea that someday someone would come to me with a mystery and I would open up the notebook and all the clues would already be there.

My mother told me that another name for detective was P.I. and that this was the word for a number that no one could ever finish writing. I said, 'What if you wrote all day and all night and never slept for a hundred years?'

'Even then,' my mother said, 'you wouldn't be done.'

About the bat, I wanted to know: Why was the darkness in a basket? Why did the moon hide from the bat? How did the badger hurt his paw? What do bats eat? Where did the darkness run? What happened to the dogs and wolves that started everything?

'Bats eat fruit and insects mostly,' my mother said. 'The darkness ran everywhere at once.'

'Do bats eat people?'

'No,' she said. 'But there's a kind in South America that drinks the blood of sleeping things. Sometimes they bite people without even waking them because their touch is as light as a kiss.'

My mother turned off the light and closed the door. The room became its night self then, full of deep corners that swallowed up the dark. Shadows moved across the wall, chasing the lights of cars. I closed my eyes and tried to dream in another language. My mother knew five languages by heart and could dream in three. Her father had been a linguist and once she had wanted to be one too. Sometimes she spent all night translating what one person in her dream said to another. When she woke up, she was so tired she could barely speak. That was why she slept all day and wandered around the house at night.

In Africa, my mother said, there is a secret city where no one ever sleeps. If a traveler stumbles upon it and falls asleep, he will be buried alive before he wakes. The villagers have never seen sleep before and would think he had died in the night. If he woke up while he was being buried, they would think he was a demon and beat him to death. The only sign you have entered the sleepless city is a certain unceasing murmuring even in the dead of night. Otherwise, it looks like every other place. Travelers are advised to wander through each city, asking passersby, 'Where can I sleep?' because in the sleepless city no one knows the answer.

My mother had taught me a little French. 'What is your name?' I knew and 'Please, can you help me find . . .?' Once I'd asked my mother to teach me Swahili and she said, 'You already know one word. Can you guess what it is?' I had guessed 'detective,' but this had been wrong. 'Safari,' she said. 'It's an old Swahili word for travel.' This was the word for the shows my father liked to watch on TV. 'Yes,' my mother said. 'That's exactly right.'

Later I wrote 'safari' in my notebook next to the word 'Sophie,' the name of my mother's other daughter, the one who died in Africa before I was born. Once I asked her if Sophie could speak Swahili before she died, but my mother said she had been too little to speak anything at all.

Another time, my mother told me that when I was born every language in the world was in my head, waiting to take form. I could have spoken Swahili or Urdu or

4

Cantonese, but now it was too late. 'Where did all the words go?' I asked.

'They just wasted away,' my mother explained, 'like a leg you never walk on.'

My mother kept a notebook too; hers was black with shiny rings. I had torn a page from it and hidden it under my bed. Sometimes when I couldn't sleep, I took the page out of its hiding place and read it:

Zero order –
Betwixt trumpeter pebbly complication vigorous tipple careen obscure attractive consequence expedition unpunished prominence chest sweetly basin awake photographer ungrateful.

First order –
Tea realizing most so the together home and for were wanted to concert I he her it the walked.

Second order –
Sun was nice dormitory is I like chocolate cake but I think that book is he wants to school there.

Third order –
Family was large dark animal came roaring down the middle of my friends love books passionately every kiss is fine.

Fourth order –
Went to the movies with a man I used to go toward Harvard Square in Cambridge is mad fun for.

Fifth order –
Road in the country was insane especially in dreary rooms where they have some books to buy for studying Greek.

Sixth order —
Easy if you know how to crochet you can make a simple scarf if they
knew the color that it.

Prose text —
More attention has been paid to diet but mostly in relation to
disease and to the growth of young children.

A moth flew into the room and fluttered against the shade. I wondered if this might be the same moth that had tried to fly to a star. But that moth had died, I remembered, or maybe it was the moth who had stayed home and circled the street lamp. My mother had told me that story too and said the moral was that stars could not be trusted and moved farther away, the closer you came. 'Poor moth,' I said again and again that day until my father put down the paper and asked me to stop. Later he explained that the nearest star was ninety-three million miles away and this made it unlikely that anyone, a person or a moth, would ever go there. When I asked what the name of the nearest star was, my father said, 'The Sun, of course.'

But my mother said that that was only one way to think of it and that in some places (Africa, for instance) people knew how to leave their bodies and fly up to the edge of the sky, where they hovered like birds. The trick, she said, was not to look down at your body in the bed, or you might lose your nerve and fall.

I looked for the moth again, but it was gone. Outside my window, slow stars moved across the sky. I could feel myself falling asleep, into sleep, it seemed. This happened when the darkness in the corner pulled me to it like water to a drain. I closed my eyes and waited. Around me, the night buzzed like a fluorescent light. *J'ai perdu mon chapeau*, I dreamed. Something brushed across my cheek and I thought it was the bat, but when I opened my eyes, there was only my mother, kneeling beside me with her hands like fur.

2

There was a lake in town that stretched all the way to Canada. This was my mother's favorite place, except in the summer, when the city people came. Then it was useless, she said. It was hardly a lake at all. By day, the water swarmed with swimmers, and at night, fireworks hid the stars.

In the summer, I tried to forget the lake, but still it was there just beyond the trees, I knew. If I wanted to go, I had to get up very early and walk with my mother in the cold dark. She didn't like to talk along the way. Instead, she shone her flashlight across the sand and to the trees. During the night, every footprint had vanished; only the tracks of birds remained. As soon as the sun came up, old men with metal detectors appeared.

These men combed the dirtiest part of the beach, just beyond the pier. There was a place there for bonfires, and charred wood spotted the shore. Half-eaten sandwiches floated in on waves. Birds dive-bombed for the bread and for the Alka-Seltzer tablets kids lined up in rows along the sand. I'd been told that if a bird swallowed one, it would explode in midair, though I had never seen this happen. My mother picked up the tablets and put them in her pockets to throw away at home. Often she forgot, and once, in a rainstorm, her coat began to hiss and fizz.

In the fall, it was different. The lake was empty again and the birds circled high above, never touching down. Every day after school, my mother and I went down to the shore to collect shells and little stones. Orange stones were best, but these were hard to find. If I found one small enough, I put it under my tongue for safekeeping. The rest I collected in my silver pail. There was a little hole at the bottom of the pail where the metal had rusted through. If a stone fell out, I couldn't pick it up again, no matter what color it was. This was a rule I had made that could never be broken. The best stone I'd ever found had been lost this way. It was small and orange with a black rim around it like the sun. Sometimes, just before I fell asleep, I thought about the way it had looked in my hand.

Often we walked to the end of the beach without talking. This was the silence game, the one my mother liked best. At first, it was hard to keep quiet, but soon I'd forget what I'd wanted to say. Instead, I pretended I was a wolf who had never said a word before and never would. I thought my mother might do this too because of the way she liked to crouch and run along the shore. The lake was very dark and deep and sometimes when I was a wolf it whispered to me in a secret way. Lake, the voice said. Lake, Lake.

There was a monster in this lake, but I had never seen it. Only my mother and six other people had. She had seen the monster one afternoon when she was out boating with her first love. Her first love's name was Michael and he was one of the seven people too. They had seen it in 1973, she said, when everyone else was inside watching TV. 'The word for such a thing is "uncanny",' she told me, and this meant that it was both familiar and strange at the same time, like the moon.

My mother always carried a newspaper clipping about that day with her. It was torn and yellow from being folded and refolded so many times. Whenever we went to the lake, she read it to me. I would have liked to hold the clipping and read it myself, but she never let me.

One day in early June 1973, Michael Maller and a friend were enjoying the tranquil beauty of Lake Champlain when they noticed the water begin to seethe. Then, to their disbelief, a head and a long willowy neck emerged, curving above a dark, floating mass. This, they realized, was no fish.

Almost paralyzed with fear, Maller nonetheless managed to aim his camera at the creature and take a quick snapshot. The result was a clear photograph of an apparently animate object, gray-brown in color and with serpentine features.

Some time later a public hearing was held in Montpelier to support the passage of legislation to protect the creature. Attending the session, Maller fervently declared: 'I just want you to know that Champ is out there. Believe me, Champ is there!'

My mother always read the last part in a silly deep voice to make me laugh. Where was Michael now, I asked, but she didn't know. She had only one photo of him, which she kept in her wallet inside a plastic sleeve. It had been taken on a honey farm in Texas, she said, the summer they drove across the country in just one week. She had shown me this picture so many times I could close my eyes and see it. There was a field full of white cabinets, each with four

10

drawers. On top of each cabinet was a rock and around the field was a wire fence. The sky behind the fence was bright blue with a tear in the corner where the sun should be. A tall, dark-haired man stood by an open drawer, his beard covered in bees. And this was Michael.

That was the last picture ever taken of him. Five days later, he disappeared in the desert. By the time they found his car, heat had warped the vinyl roof. The windows were down and the floorboards were covered with sand. On the front seat was his driver's license, a map of America, and a twenty-dollar bill. This had been in California, my mother said, in a place called Joshua Tree.

'Where did he go?' I asked, though she always said different things. (In the past, she had told me: Mexico, Milwaukee, the moon.)

My mother put the picture back inside its sleeve. 'I think he became a cryptozoologist,' she said. 'There was a monster in the Congo he was desperate to see.' She smoothed out the clipping in her hands. 'Do Sea Serpents Have Rights?' the headline said.

Cryptozoologists were detectives who specialized in finding hidden animals, I knew. This was the sort of detective my mother wanted me to be. The people who investigated the Loch Ness monster were cryptozoologists, and so were the people in search of Bigfoot.

My mother had given me a book called *The Encyclopedia of the Unexplained*, which listed all the monsters of the world alphabetically. 'A' was for the Abominable Snowman that lived in the mountains of Nepal and walked upright like a man. No bullet could kill it, the book said, though it yelped like a puppy when shot.

My mother said most cryptozoologists were really just

hunters in disguise, but that there were some, a very few, who worked like secret agents in the wild. These were the ones who found lost animals and helped them hide.

'You see these men in the paper sometimes,' she said. 'The secret ones. And they are always very sure of themselves, delighted to prove it's all a hoax. It was no more than a moose, they say. Just a fallen log or common bear. They're very convincing, these men, but their smiles give them away. There's not a man alive that smiles when he's wrong.'

She took the Polaroid camera out of her purse and walked down to the water. Every time we came to the lake, she took a picture, just in case. The trick was to aim at something else so that you caught the monster by surprise.

She stood in the water and aimed at the far pier. There was a click and a whir as the picture came out. I looked at the lake. It was almost dark. In the distance, something shimmered and moved away. My mother turned the picture face-down and gave it to me. She never looked until the end, but I didn't like to wait. In the beginning, everything was gray, then slowly this faded and dim shapes emerged. This was the moment when the monster might appear. A fin might rise to the surface or a hump or a head.

I waited, holding my breath. Then the water came in, and the sky and the pier. I held the picture up to the light, but there was nothing to see. Only the dark skin of the lake and the birds circling round. 'One more for the drawer,' my mother said.

At home, we had a special drawer that we kept the pictures in. Inside were dozens of photographs, numbered and filed by date. Two years' worth. Number 37 was the best. It showed a dark black spot hovering just above the lake. It could be the monster or it could be my mother's thumb. Only an expert could tell for sure.

Sometimes my mother tired of looking for the monster and we'd go to the park instead. The rule about the park was that we could only go there if we went in disguise. Otherwise, men might stop and talk to us. Men were always trying to talk to my mother, it seemed. But, in disguise, we could travel incognito. That was the way spies traveled, she said.

My mother knew a lot about spies and sometimes hinted that she had been one once. She knew a way, for example, to make an umbrella shoot a poison dart. Also that the CIA had tried to kill the President of Cuba with an exploding clam. She showed me how to send secret messages by underlining words in a newspaper and dropping it on a bench.

Someone is after you, was the message we left the man in the park who wore sharkskin boots and shooed the birds away.

Meet me on the moon, we left for the old woman with the flowered hat and walking stick.

Many admire you, we left for the one-eyed dog walker and his six basset hounds.

Sometimes I tried to guess which of my mother's stories were true and which were not, but I was usually wrong. Even my father knew about the exploding clam, it turned out, though he grew vague when asked about the poisoned umbrella. 'My wife, Mata Hari,' was all he'd say.

The day before Thanksgiving, there was a terrible storm. One moment there was a sharp chill in the air, and the next, ice fell down. All afternoon, my father peered out the window, checking the roads. That night they were going to a benefit to raise money for the raptor center where my mother worked. *This party's for the birds!* the invitations said.

I sat on the edge of the bathtub and watched my mother put on her face. Outside, the trees were breaking themselves into pieces. Ice tapped against the glass. My mother went to the window and rubbed away the steam. 'Listen, Grace,' she said, 'I think someone's speaking to us in code.' I looked out the window. There was nothing but the dark trees to see. My mother tapped twice on the glass, then cupped a hand to her ear. For a long time she stood like that, waiting. Then she gave up and walked away. I wanted to ask her if she had really been a spy, but I was too afraid. If I told you that, I'd have to kill you, she said once.

My mother held a finger to her lips. Loose lips sink ships, she liked to say. I watched her put her eyelashes on. If she touched them to my cheek, this meant a butterfly had kissed me.

From my bedroom window, I watched as my parents struggled down the icy walk. My mother was wearing her mermaid dress, the one with the blue scales. My father had on his funeral suit. By the old car, they stopped and kissed. Ice fell all around them, tiny silver shards that caught the light. When my mother opened her umbrella, my father ducked.

3

That night on TV, I saw a man pull a train down the tracks with just his teeth. He put his mouth in a bit like a horse, then he walked backwards and pulled as hard as he could. The train inched forward. It was a small silver train with red trim. The man clenched his teeth and pulled again. This went on for some time.

'Where is he taking that train?' I wanted to know. 'Is there anyone inside it?'

My baby-sitter didn't answer. His name was Edgar and he only answered questions that interested him. He had told me this on the first day we met. On that day, he had answered a question about the temperature of the Sun, but had refused to tell me his age or height.

Later I found out from my father that Edgar was sixteen and a boy genius who worked in the laboratory downtown. He was very tall and wore sandals made of rope. Once he had been a student at my father's school, but then he had written a paper that had revolutionized the study of poisonous molds.

I liked Edgar even though he ignored me. He was paid five dollars an hour to watch me and I thought that he must spend this money on soap. My mother said she had never seen a boy with such clean hands. It was as if he wasn't really a boy at all.

Sometimes he washed his hands four or five times in one night and he always brought his own soap with him. His soap came in a big black square and smelled like roses. He carried it in a plastic bag in the outside pocket of his coat. Once I asked if I could try his soap, but he said I would ruin it if I did.

Mostly, Edgar liked to stay inside and read. He did not like to dig holes or catch bees as I did. 'You go ahead,' he'd say. 'I'll be right out.' But often he'd forget and it would grow dark outside as I waited.

Edgar had promised to build a robot that would play badminton in the yard with me. There was an old net in the basement, and when the robot was done, I could set it up outside and play, he said. This robot would be as strong as ten men and have a special light on top of his head so we could play in the dark. Until then, I was not to ask about the net.

Edgar never answered questions about the show with the train, even though it was my favorite one. Every week, there were three stories, all of them different. After the train man, there was a story about a monk in Tibet who wanted to be locked inside a trunk and thrown to sea. This man claimed he could slow his breathing and heart at will. He took off his orange robe and curled up inside a trunk. In a previous life, he had been a bear, his mother said.

Two men came over and closed the trunk. Then they covered it with chains. It made a big splash when it was thrown overboard; then nothing happened for a long time. A clock appeared at the bottom of the screen and ticked the time away. Six minutes passed. A woman on the boat screamed. On the shore, divers in wet suits paced along the water's edge. There was the sound of someone crying. The man's mother, the announcer said. Six and a half minutes. There was a ripple in the water and then suddenly the man emerged. He held his arms above his head and waved. Everyone cheered. 'How did you get out of the trunk?' someone asked. The monk laughed. 'The real question,' he said, 'is how did the trunk get out of me?'

The electricity went off, and the TV too. 'The storm,' Edgar said. After a minute, the lights flickered, but they didn't come back on.

Even in the dark, I kept thinking about the man in the trunk. 'Why was his mother crying?' I wanted to know. 'If she knew he used to be a bear?'

Edgar was quiet. He found a candle and lit it. He turned his back to me and started to read. The book he was reading was called *Being and Nothingness*. The only question he'd answered all night long was which was better. (Nothingness.)

Later Edgar told me a story about a girl who fell into a black hole and was never found. A black hole was a collapsed star that nothing could get out of, not even light. If you fell into one, you would fall forever because there was no bottom, only endless space. This was nothingness, Edgar said, when each part of you flew into pieces no bigger than a bit of dust.

I went to the window. There was nothing to see with the streetlights out. I imagined my mother across town dancing in her mermaid dress. The year before, she had taught my father how to waltz, but he always stepped on her toes, so they never did. I've got a man with two left feet, she sang whenever he tried.

A car went by with its headlights on. Then another and

another. The neighbor's dog barked each time the street lit up. I thought of how you could quiet a bird by covering its head with a black cloth so that it would think it was night.

It was too dark inside the house. I could see Edgar across the room, but I couldn't make out his face. *He's wearing a mask*, I thought suddenly, but then I saw the shine of his eyes when he lit a match. He hummed a bit of a song I knew. The one about the woman who turned into a weeping-willow tree. 'Has anyone ever really fallen in a black hole?' I asked him. I could hear him humming in the dark, but he didn't answer.

The next morning, only my father was up. 'Your mother was the belle of the ball,' he said. 'She danced with everyone she met.' He picked up her party shoes and put them away. On the kitchen table was an empty wine glass and a pile of blue scales.

He fixed me a bowl of cereal, but there was no milk. Orange juice might be good, he suggested. I shook my head. I had once seen my father eat a raisin-and-mayonnaise sandwich when there was nothing else around. My father sighed. He made me toast. Then he went into the living room and turned on the radio. He never knew what to say when we were alone. Once, when my mother went away for a weekend, he read me an entire book about the evolution of squirrels.

On the radio, someone was singing about a devil moon. My father turned the dial. There was static and then the weatherman came on. 'After last night's storm, some residents are wondering if we've entered a new Ice Age,' he said.

'Idiot,' my father muttered. He put on his boots and

went outside. Broken branches littered the yard. He gathered them in a pile and stacked them by the shed. From the window, I watched him cleaning up.

My mother came into the room. She was in her bathrobe and her hair was all ratted up from the night before. 'Where has your father run off to?' she asked. I pointed outside. She frowned when she saw him clearing the yard. 'I suppose this means Mr. Success is still coming over?' she said.

I nodded. 'Aunt Fe and the cousins too.'

My mother put her finger to her head like a gun. 'Kill me now,' she said.

I pretended to shoot myself too, but really I was happy they were coming. The summer before, my Uncle Pete had given me a trick pack of gum that snapped shut on anyone who tried to take a piece. I had carried it with me everywhere until my cousin Alec stole it and threw it into the lake.

Uncle Pete was older than my father by three and a half minutes. Because of this, he called my father 'Sport' and 'Kid' and sucker-punched him when they said goodbye. No matter how many times he did this, my father always looked surprised. The two of them looked just alike, except that my uncle's eyes were blue. He had once had brown eyes too, but then he had become Mr. Science on TV. Colored contacts, my mother said.

My uncle's show came on every day after school and twice on weekends. I liked to watch it because it was different every time. One day it might be about asteroids and the next about rattlesnakes. It all depended on the questions kids sent in.

My mother put on her slippers and went outside. She walked right over the frozen grass and snuck up on my father, who was scraping ice off the car. Right away they started arguing. I couldn't hear what they were saying, but I could tell he was trying to get her to put on a coat.

When my mother came back inside, the hem of her bathrobe was covered with frost. She went into the kitchen and started cooking. 'Yams!' I heard her say. 'Dinner rolls! Pie!'

I went into the dining room to play with the toothpick replica of the *Mayflower* I had made. Inside was a small army of toy soldiers painted black-and-white to look like pilgrims. Even painted, it was hard to tell what they were because of their parachutes and guns. Look out, Indians, my mother said when I showed it to her.

She called Edgar and invited him over for dinner. His parents had gone to Europe for the holidays, but he had stayed home to study a particularly luminous form of mold. For weeks now, he had been trying to light a lamp with it.

I went upstairs and listened on the extension. My mother was talking about candied yams. 'But my hands are glowing,' Edgar said. 'I haven't slept in forty-eight hours.'

'We'll expect you at five,' my mother told him. She hung up the phone, but Edgar stayed on the line. 'I know you're there, Grace,' he said; then he clicked off too.

In the kitchen, my mother was peeling potatoes. She had gotten dressed and twisted her hair into a knot. 'Where's the turkey?' I asked her.

'In the oven,' she said.

I opened the door to make sure. The year before, my mother had given away our turkey to a woman begging outside the supermarket. No one knew she had done this until Thanksgiving dinner when she served a bucket of chicken instead.

The doorbell rang. 'Now, who could that be?' my mother asked.

I looked through the peephole and there was Edgar, carrying a bulky package wrapped in brown paper and masking tape. He was wearing a suit and tie, but still had his rope sandals on.

I let him in. 'What did you bring?' I asked. Edgar ignored me and took off his coat. He set the package down on the dining-room table. 'Mrs. Davitt?' he called.

My mother came in from the kitchen, wiping her hands on her skirt. 'You're much too early,' she told Edgar. 'Nothing's ready yet.' She reached out to straighten his tie, which had come undone.

Edgar waved her hand away. 'I have something to show you.' He moved around the table, setting the package upright. 'I've done it,' he announced. 'It took eight weeks, but I figured it out.'

'Done what?' my mother said.

Edgar didn't answer. Instead, he carefully began unwinding the tape.

I stood on a chair to get a better view. The package was shaped like a giant mushroom and I felt certain that this was what it contained.

It took a long time for Edgar to get the tape off. 'We don't have all day,' my mother said, tapping her fingers on the table. She took off her shoe and shook something out of it.

Edgar now tore at the tape feverishly. *'Voilà!'* he said, ripping open the package. Inside was an ordinary table lamp.

'Well?' my mother said.

Edgar held a finger to his lips. He went to the window

and pulled the curtain shut. In the dark room, the lamp began to glow with an odd blue light.

'What is it?' I asked him.

Edgar took the shade off the lamp. 'It's a rare form of luminous mold,' he explained. 'Generally found in Arctic regions where there is little or no sun.'

My mother leaned forward to study the flickering light. The blue glow made her look as if she was underwater. 'How marvelous,' she said. 'What do you plan to do with it?'

Edgar closed his eyes. He had a dream, he told her, that one day entire cities might be illuminated by mold.

4

L ater Edgar fell asleep at the dining-room table. This was one of Edgar's talents. He could fall asleep anywhere. 'Leave him be,' my mother said when I tried to wake him. She wrapped up the mold lamp and put it away. While Edgar slept, I surrounded his feet with pilgrim soldiers. Some wanted to shoot him, but others hoped to keep him as a pet. Before this could be decided, Edgar woke with a start to the sound of a car in the driveway. 'Who's there?' he mumbled, kicking over the pilgrims all at once.

I ran around to the front of the house. Alec was standing on the sidewalk wearing his black magician's cape. He had on the shirt I liked best. 'Super Duper Popcorn Freak,' it said on the front. Sometimes when he visited, he pretended to give me the shirt, but he always took it back at the end of the day.

My aunt and uncle unloaded the car trunk, which was filled with groceries.

'Come give me a kiss, Grace,' Aunt Fe said. She was wearing a complicated outfit in shades of orange and brown. Once she had sold real estate, but then she had decided to become a color consultant. Everywhere she went, she carried swatches of different colors so that she could figure out what season you were. I was a spring, she said, and she was a fall.

I let her kiss my cheek. She smelled like cinnamon. Men like the smell of cinnamon more than any perfume on earth, she'd told me once.

I squirmed out of her arms. 'Where's Mary?' I said.

'Still in the car. She's having a time-out.'

'What did she do?'

My aunt shook her head.

'She stabbed Alec with a fork,' my uncle said cheerfully.

I peered at Mary through the window. Her eyes were closed and her hands were folded as if in prayer.

'What's she doing?'

'Praying for deliverance, I suspect,' my uncle said. He handed me a casserole wrapped in foil.

We carried all the food inside. My mother met us at the door with a kiss. 'Pete, Fe, lovely to see you,' she said. She went into the kitchen and checked on the turkey. My uncle watched her from the doorway. If I squinted, I could make him look like my father, but whenever I did this, it made my head hurt. He came up behind my mother and whispered something in her ear. She smiled, but she didn't speak to him.

'Anna, Anna, Anna,' he said. 'Are you ever going to forgive me?'

My mother made him a drink with an umbrella, a sword, and two olives in it. 'A peace offering,' she said. She had only just started speaking to him again. When my uncle didn't pick me to be on his show, my mother gave him the silent treatment for weeks. If he called, she hung up on him. If he came over, she didn't say a word. One night, after he'd gone on and on about the authentic Japanese garden he planned to build, my mother snuck into his backyard and filled his new pagoda with garden gnomes. Be reasonable, Anna, my father said.

In the next room, my father put on a record. I could hear him talking to Aunt Fe about colors. He was explaining something to her about the spectrum of light, but she kept interrupting him. My father was a winter.

'Go, Daddy-o,' the man on the record yelled. My uncle took my mother in his arms and danced with her. She put her head to his chest and sniffed his shirt.

'Your personal hygiene has gone to pot since you became a celebrity, Pete,' she told him.

My uncle laughed. 'It's not my fault. I was born without a sense of smell. You're half hound dog, I think.'

My mother spun out of his grasp. She looked pretty, dancing. 'Drinks, everyone,' she called.

Aunt Fe came in, carrying a bowl of peanuts.

'How goes it with the birds?' she asked my mother. She was wearing a flowered scarf that kept slipping off her shoulders. It fell on the floor and I picked it up.

My mother sighed. 'One of the last two dusky seaside sparrows in the world died last week. The surviving bird has no mate, so for all intents and purposes that species is extinct.'

'Isn't that a shame.' Aunt Fe opened the oven door and looked inside. 'I'm glad to see our bird's not on the endangered list this year,' she said.

My mother looked vaguely out the window. 'Where has Edgar disappeared to?' she asked me.

I found him on the back porch with Alec. Alec had a deck of cards and was showing him a trick. 'Pick a card, any card,' he said.

Edgar picked a card.

'Now put it back in the deck without showing me.'

Edgar did this as well.

With a flourish, Alec shuffled the deck, then turned over the top card. 'Is this your card, sir?' he asked.

Edgar shook his head.

Alec frowned and turned over the next one. 'Perhaps this is the card you have chosen?' he asked.

'No, it is not,' Edgar said.

Alec began flipping over cards faster and faster. Jack of hearts, queen of spades, seven of diamonds, five of clubs.

'No, no, a thousand times no,' Edgar said. He picked up his book and went inside. Alec followed him, but Edgar closed the screen door between them. 'Before you ply your trade again, I suggest you master the sleight of hand required,' he told him.

After Edgar left, Alec threw the pack of cards into the driveway. 'What are you looking at?' he asked me. Then he went back inside too.

I gathered up the cards and examined them. Some had small folds on the corners, and one was marked on the back with an X. After a while, Mary came out and sat beside me. It was time for dinner, she said. She tilted her head and looked at me critically. 'You should brush your hair better,' she told me. 'The part is crooked and it sticks out on the sides.'

Grooming was important to Mary because she believed her portrait would one day appear on a dollar bill. The summer before, she had sent away in the mail for a kit to start her own country. Marydom, it was going to be called. It wasn't ready yet because there was a lot of paperwork to do, she said.

She took out a brush and ran it over my hair roughly. She

brushed my ears and forehead too. Finally, she put it down. 'I give up. You're hopeless,' she told me. She went inside and I followed her. 'There you are, silly girls,' my mother said.

Before dinner, Aunt Fe said a blessing, even though my father asked her not to. He didn't believe in blessings or in any kind of religion at all. It was just superstition, he said. But Aunt Fe insisted on saying grace because it was Thanksgiving. She closed her eyes and asked everyone at the table to tell something they were thankful for. There was a long silence. Then Aunt Fe said she was thankful for the bounty of America. My mother was thankful for our family, and Uncle Pete was thankful that no one had given our turkey away. No one else was thankful for anything except for Mary, who muttered something about being treasurer of the fifth grade.

My father seated Edgar at the kids' end of the table, between Mary and me. As soon as he sat down, Mary wagged her finger at him. 'I saw you,' she said. 'You had your eyes open during grace.'

Edgar didn't answer. He took all his silverware off the table and wiped it carefully with the napkin in his lap.

'I saw you,' Mary said again.

Edgar stared at his plate. He cut his turkey into neat quarters and ate it. Then he ate his cranberry sauce, then his stuffing, then his roll. When all the other food was gone, he ate one miniature marshmallow and one yam.

Mary poked him in the ribs. 'Are you an orphan?' she asked.

Edgar sighed. He put his head in his hands.

'Is everything all right?' my mother called from her end of the table.

'Just perfect, Mrs. Davitt,' he said.

After dessert, Edgar excused himself. He thanked my mother for dinner and took his leave with a small bow.

'He's an odd duck, isn't he?' my aunt said after he left. 'And those shoes!'

My mother sidestepped her and closed the door. 'Edgar made those shoes himself,' she said.

We went into the den to watch a tape of my uncle's show. It was the season finale and no one had seen it yet. I sat up close to the TV with Alec. My father wandered in and out of the room, doing things. He bundled up the newspapers and took them outside. He changed a lightbulb and put away the mail. Then he oiled the place in the door that always caught. 'Sit down. You're driving everyone crazy,' my mother said.

My father sat down on the window ledge away from everyone. He tossed a tennis ball back and forth from hand to hand. My uncle stood at the front of the room and introduced the tape. He showed us a picture of him shaking hands with the mayor of New York City. Then one of him kissing a beauty queen. Finally, he sat down and turned on the TV. 'Here goes,' he said. 'Remember, kids, let Mr. Science know what you think.'

The theme music came on. There was a picture of the sun and then of an old man walking through a field of corn. The man had on overalls and a hat made of straw. He walked and walked without saying a word. Above him, the sky was a blinding blue. When the man reached the end of the field, he tore off an ear of corn and held it to the light. One side was bright yellow, but the other was spotted black. For a moment, I thought the man might cry, but he just threw the spotted corn back into the field. 'Too much sun can be as harmful as too little,' my uncle said.

Mary came over and sat beside me. 'What's this one about?' she whispered.

'Corn,' I said.

'It can't just be corn. It has to be something educational.'

'It's just corn.'

The question girl came out, carrying a steaming platter. My uncle took an ear of corn and bit into it delicately.

'See,' I said.

The question girl smiled and took the platter away. She was about my age and had curly blond hair that she wore piled on top of her head like a queen. Two hundred kids had tried out for her part, but she had been picked because she'd explained the theory of relativity while twirling around on roller skates.

The question girl stepped forward and began to speak in her smiling way. My uncle stood just outside the spotlight.

ARE WE THE ONLY ANIMALS THAT GROW
OUR OWN FOOD?
Humans are the only animals intelligent enough to farm. Until the Neolithic Age, people lived as hunters and gatherers, often traveling great distances to find food. But then, around 8000 B.C., agriculture was invented. Experts believe that people in the Middle East were the first to discover that seeds from wild grains could be planted and harvested. This probably came about when a woman gathering food noticed that new shoots had grown from spilled grain. If it hadn't been for the discovery of this sharp-eyed lass, we might still be following our dinner from place to place.

The tape stopped. Everyone applauded. 'Wait,' my uncle said. 'That's not the end.' He got up and fiddled with the TV; then he turned and saw my father with the remote control. 'Okay, kid, what's the problem?' he asked.

My father cleared his throat. He rewound the tape a little ways. 'Are we the only animals that grow our own food?' the question girl asked. 'Humans are the only animals intelligent enough to farm,' my uncle said.

My father paused the tape on the last word. 'It's just that, strictly speaking, that isn't true,' he said. 'There seems to be a small error in your research here.'

My uncle got up and poured himself a drink. When he turned around, his face was red. He smiled at my father. 'Care to explain what the hell you're talking about, Jonathan?' he said.

Aunt Fe put a hand on his arm. She gestured in our direction. Uncle Pete closed his eyes. 'What the heck you're talking about, I mean.'

My father leapt up from his chair. He went to the bookcase and took down a book called *The Big Book of Ants*.

'Ants!' my mother said happily.

My father opened the book. His hands shook a little as he looked for the passage he wanted. 'Ah, here it is,' he said and began to read.

Over one hundred and ninety species of ants have been found to grow a kind of fungi which they fertilize, plant, and even prune. Many of them also keep aphids the way we keep cows. They milk them to obtain their sweet honeydew and build shelters for them like barns. One kind of ant, the fierce Amazon, goes so far as to steal the larvae of other ants to keep as slaves. These slave ants build homes for and feed the Amazon ants, who are unable to do anything but fight. The soldier ants depend completely on their slave ants for survival. Without them, they would die.

My father closed the book. 'I just wanted to alert you, Peter. I thought it would save you the embarrassment of receiving corrective letters.' He held out the book, but my uncle waved it away.

'I doubt even among my one million viewers there are many ant experts.'

My mother laughed. 'Oh, Jonathan's hardly an expert. You're the one who always says he never amounted to much.'

My uncle got up and announced he was going for a walk. But as soon as he got outside, we heard the car start. It roared out of the driveway and into the street. My father mumbled something and shook his head. I wondered if my uncle might be communicating with him telepathically. Identical twins could do this, I had read in *The Encyclopedia of the Unexplained*. Sometimes when my father was talking to my uncle he'd shake his head violently as if a message was coming through.

The pause button on the TV went off and there was the sound of applause. Alec clicked through the channels one by one. He stopped on a commercial featuring a singing toilet seat and hummed along. 'Don't be an idiot,' Mary said.

My mother went into the kitchen and I followed her. When my father passed by, she made a face at him. 'Without them, they would die,' she said in her silly deep voice. My father laughed, holding his stomach. 'Stop that,' he told her, but he didn't mean it. Every time she said it, he laughed again.

5

The day he proposed, my father took my mother to see King Tut's tomb in Egypt. It was their first vacation together. For days beforehand, my father was so nervous he couldn't eat. On the way to the airport, he fainted and ran off the road. My mother took the wheel and steered them to a stop. In the tall grass, my father lay with his head on the dashboard like a dead man. My mother took the ice from her drink and touched it to his wrists and neck. She pricked his fingers with a safety pin. When my father finally came to, he started the car and drove off without a word. Are you all right, my mother asked him. Just fine, my father said. They drove on in silence. Clouds of dust filled the air. Halfway to the airport, my father discovered his pinpricked hand. I thought I was dreaming, he said.

In the Valley of the Kings, they waited in line for hours and he took a picture of her posed in profile like an Egyptian queen. Once inside, my mother tried to cut off a small piece of the mummy's wrapping and set off an alarm. A guard came and escorted her into a back room. When they finally let her go, she was not allowed to keep the Band-Aid-sized piece of cloth she had snipped off with her sewing scissors. Later, beside the pyramids, my father got down on one knee and said, I want to marry you, Anna.

You're the only woman I've ever met who never bores me.

Afterwards, my mother insisted they go dancing to celebrate. They found a little café at the end of a winding street. There was wine there and a small band. An old man taught my mother a complicated Egyptian dance. You are very beautiful, he said. My father sat alone at the bar, watching them. His feet were covered with blisters from the long walk to the pyramids. The band began to play faster, then faster still. My mother came over and took his hand. Dance with me, she said, and my father did. Later, at the hotel, when she took off his shoes, she was surprised to find them filled with blood.

My mother had a scrapbook that she'd kept from the trip. On the first page was the picture of her as a queen, and a postcard she had saved from King Tut. The postcard showed a pile of gold jewelry and a mummified cat with a pink tongue. It was the sweetest thing you've ever seen, my mother always said about the cat. Once she told me about the curse that had befallen everyone who disturbed the king's tomb. One of the explorers had had his canary devoured by a cobra the day after he unsealed the chamber. Another had died of an insect bite to the face. The night that this happened, the man's dog, who was thousands of miles away, let out a terrible howl and dropped dead. But the worst was the very last. There was a woman explorer on the trip and she alone seemed to have escaped harm. Twenty years passed without incident. Then one morning she went up to the attic and hung herself with a piece of laundry line. The note she left behind said: 'I have succumbed to a curse that has forced me to depart from this life.' This was my favorite part of the story and my mother indulged me by telling it again and again. 'And to think,' she said, 'that this woman was a scientist just like your father!'

Sometimes I worried that the curse would fall on our family too. But my father said that this was just superstition. Superstition was when you believed in supernatural powers, I knew. It was crossing your fingers for luck or not stepping on a crack or going to church to pray for your soul.

I had never been to church because my father had vowed to raise me a heathen. A heathen was a godless thing, my mother explained. In some parts of America, it was against the law to be one. On Sundays, I watched from the woods as the Christians drove by. The women had on dresses and the men wore dark suits. Sometimes I threw rocks at their cars and waited to see what God would do. Nothing much, it turned out.

One of the cars that passed by every Sunday belonged to my teacher, Mrs. Carr. She always wore a hat and gloves and looked straight ahead as she drove. I was careful to hide behind the trees so she wouldn't see me. I had an idea that she didn't like to be watched. Sometimes when she wrote on the board, her fingers trembled violently. As soon as she sat down, she'd clasp them together and hide them beneath her desk.

I was a little afraid of her. She was so old her skin was transparent, and one of her eyes was clouded over like milk. My mother told me that she lived all alone in a dome-shaped house at the edge of the lake. Her husband had built it for her and it was supposed to be powered by the sun, but sometimes it didn't work. When it rained, Mrs. Carr brought blankets and a pillow and slept in the nurse's office at school. In her purse she carried a small radio so she could listen to the weather reports. 'Shh,' she'd say, holding it to her ear. 'I think there's a storm front coming in.'

Twice already that year, I had made her cry. Once when I stole her radio and once when I told her I didn't believe in God. 'What a terrible thing to say, Grace,' she said. 'Don't you realize you're named after God's greatest gift of all?' That night, when I asked my father if this was true, he called Mrs. Carr an ignorant fool. He threw down the paper and paced around the room. 'Calm down, Jonathan,' my mother told him, but it was too late. Already he'd dragged the phone into the living room.

I knew my father was going to call Mrs. Carr and read to her from his favorite book. The book was called *Know Your Constitution!* and my father carried it with him everywhere. This was the book he quoted from whenever he wrote to the newspaper.

My mother got up from the table and closed the door. 'Poor woman,' she said.

In the next room, my father was yelling something. 'Perhaps you are unfamiliar with the separation of church and state,' I heard him say.

The next day my father gave me a copy of the book to give to Mrs. Carr. Don't be tedious, Jonathan, my mother said, but he slipped it in my backpack anyway.

When I gave her the book, Mrs. Carr frowned and put it away in a bottom drawer. I told her that I had been named after my mother's aunt, who had red hair and choked on a biscuit when she was just twenty-one. 'Is that so?' Mrs. Carr said.

After lunch, she gave me back my 'Ways to Be Safe' paper with red marks all over it. We were supposed to write about the policeman who had visited our school last week, but I had written about *The Encyclopedia of the Unexplained* instead. I told about the man in California who was struck dead when a hunk of meat fell from the sky, and the woman in Texas who burst into flames on top of a Ferris wheel. Also the baby in Oregon who was born half chicken, half boy, and pecked his mother to death.

F. You have not followed the assignment, Mrs. Carr wrote.

A girl came over and asked me what I got on my paper. Her name was Darcy Edwards, but I called her Girl 8 secretly. This was because of something Edgar had said. One day he rode by my school at recess and saw me standing alone by the fence. He stopped to talk to me and we watched the other kids playing for a while. All the boys were shooting marbles and all the girls were jumping rope. Then all the girls moved to the swings and all the boys played whiffle ball. Edgar spun the pedals on his bike. 'Did you ever think that everyone around you might be an ingenious robot and you're the only one that's not?' he asked. In fact, I had never thought this, but now I saw it could be true. It explained why all the girls knew how to play the clapping game and all the boys brought baseball cards to school. The next day, I changed all my classmates' names to numbers to better reflect their metal hearts.

'What did you get?' Girl 8 asked again. I covered the grade with my hands. 'An A,' I told her. She snatched the paper away from me. 'I knew you were lying,' she said. Later I stole her snowflake mittens and hid them inside my desk.

6

J ust before Christmas, Mrs. Carr arranged a field trip to the raptor center where my mother worked. The day of the bird tour, I got up very early and drove with my mother on the highway out of town. She had brought along a box of slides and as she drove she held them up to the light and looked at them. When we got to the center, I sat in the lobby and waited for the rest of my class to arrive. On the bulletin board, there was a sign that said:

50 Javan Rhinoceros
30 California Condors
18 Mauritian Pink Pigeons
12 Chatham Island Robins
6 Mauritian Kestrels
5 Javan Tigers
3 Kauai O-O-Honeyeaters
2 Dusky Seaside Sparrows
1 Abingdon Galapagos Tortoise

Once my father had given me an old map that showed the world supported by a series of tortoises one on top of the other. 'That was the way people thought of the Earth back then,' he explained. 'Before they had sailed all the way around the world and seen that it was round.' At the

37

bottom of the pyramid was a tremendous turtle with a weathered purple shell. This one I thought had survived.

My mother went to the bulletin board and crossed out a line. There was only one dusky seaside sparrow in the world left now, she said, and it lived all alone in a cage in Disney World. She turned away so I couldn't see her face. It was early still and the sky was gray. My mother closed her eyes. 'Can we go see that bird?' I asked her. I knew about Disney World, about all the other things that were there. My mother turned to look at me. I made my face look sad. 'We'll see,' she said.

My mother's job at the center was to take care of the baby birds. At night, people left them in the parking lot in shoe boxes and shopping bags. BIRD, they wrote in block letters on the front. Most of them were not raptors, but she took them anyway. There were four in the center now. Eeny, Meeny, Miney, and Moe. Two were ospreys and two were sparrows. Only the ospreys were birds of prey, my mother said. Their heads were covered with white fuzz like the heads of old men. They had black wings and sharp, leathery claws that were bright yellow. The sparrows were dull brown and cried all the time. My mother fed them with eye droppers and sang them to sleep.

In her office, there was a picture of her, knee deep in water, dressed as a giant crane. The summer before, she had gone to Texas and worked for a program that bred captive whooping cranes. All the workers dressed as birds so that the cranes would know how to feed their own babies when they were set free. My mother took the costume with her when she left and sometimes she put on the feathered head and talked through the beak to me.

The clock struck eight. 'Where is everyone?' my mother

said. I went outside and waited for the bus. At a quarter after, it arrived, and all the kids got off and milled around the parking lot. Mrs. Carr motioned for me to get in line. Girls 1–9 already were. My mother clapped her hands. 'Let's begin,' she said. She led us down the hall and into a small auditorium. 'Quiet, children,' Mrs. Carr whispered, holding a finger to her lips. My mother stepped behind a podium at the front of the room. Above her, a screen showed a picture of an empty sky.

'Imagine, if you will, a world without birds,' she said. 'It may be hard to picture, yet one day this may be. In the last thousand years, fifteen hundred species of birds have become extinct. Scientists estimate only eighty-five hundred species remain. Within your lifetime, at least a hundred more will disappear.' On the screen behind her, pictures of birds that were already gone flashed by. 'The moa. The dodo. The great auk,' my mother said. Then there was a picture of thousands of birds flying in formation across the sky. These were the passenger pigeons, I knew. I hoped my mother wouldn't tell the story of what happened to them, because it always made her cry.

After the slide show, we went to the baby-bird room and my mother showed everyone the picture of when she was a crane. Then she put on a glove and brought out the hawk that sat on her hand. Mrs. Carr asked what the bird's name was and my mother said that it was Hawk. Hawk had a black hood over his head like a tiny executioner. This was so he would think it was night and not make a fuss. With Hawk on her hand, my mother led us down the hall to see the picture charts of how birds evolved from dinosaurs. This was the part the boys liked best. In school, they talked on and on about dinosaurs, their tremendous teeth and pea-sized brains. One of them had a button that said '*I killed the dinosaurs!*' and he often wore this pinned to his coat.

My mother took off Hawk's hood. The bird blinked and looked around at the bright lights. Then he made a soft sputtering sound and fluttered his wings.

'Can I tickle his feet?' Girl 4 asked.

'No, you may not,' my mother said. She put Hawk back in his cage and brought out the skeleton of a small bird. 'Birds have hollow bones,' she explained, 'which is why they are light enough to fly.' She showed us a bird's head which had been cut in half. The bones were shot through with tiny holes like a spiderweb. My mother held it up to the light and looked through to the other side. 'Isn't that extraordinary?' Mrs. Carr said.

In the lobby, my mother paused in front of the extinction sign. 'Five weeks ago, one of the last two dusky seaside sparrows in the world died,' she told the class. 'Soon they will be completely extinct.' Her hands shook a little as she pointed to the bird's name and the number beside it. I looked around to see if anyone had noticed, but no one was paying attention. Boy 6 was passing out gum and all the kids were holding out their hands to him.

My mother turned away from the sign. 'Follow me,' she said. She led everyone down the hall to a large glass case with two stuffed passenger pigeons inside. They were ordinary-looking birds, brownish gray with a spot of white on their chests.

My mother turned on the light that illuminated the case. The two birds inside had dull eyes and moth-eaten coats. They were sitting on a fake branch against a backdrop of trees. 'Once the passenger pigeon was the most numerous bird in the world. When a flock of them flew past the sun, the sky darkened as if from an eclipse.' My mother paused and looked around the room. I wondered if she was going to tell about the great hunt that killed twenty thousand of them in one day. I was very little when she first told me about this, and afterwards I crawled under the back porch and hid there until it got dark. Just before the end of the story, when she got to the part about the birds burning in the trees, my father grabbed her wrist and said, 'Can't you see you're scaring her, Anna?' but she told me the rest anyway.

But this time my mother trailed off in the middle of the story. She turned off the display light and went into the back room. When she returned, she was carrying a tray of feathers. She pointed out the different markings on them and explained how quills were made of keratin, just like fingernails. Then she passed them around for everyone to see. Some of the kids put feathers in their hair and tomahawked each other. Mrs. Carr sighed and shooed them away. Afterwards, she called for everyone to line up for the bus. I was allowed to stay behind since school got out at noon that day.

When everyone else was gone, my mother took out a handkerchief and wiped the case clean. On the wall beside the pigeons was a plaque that marked the date they'd gone extinct. Sept. 1, 1914. The last one's name was Martha, it said, and she died of old age in the Cincinnati Zoo.

7

W e went to the woods to pick out our Christmas tree. My father didn't believe in Christmas, but still we celebrated it. It was like not believing in God but still you prayed. My mother said it was a shame to cut down a tree, so instead we chose one in the forest and tied a ribbon around it so we could find it again.

On Christmas morning, we got dressed in our warmest clothes and went to see our tree. My father pulled a sled behind him with all our presents on it and we had a picnic breakfast in the snow. Pine needles fell on the coffee cake my mother had made. We opened our presents all at once because it was too cold to take turns. My mother gave my father a telescope, an old map of Africa, and a woodworking set. My father gave her a bathrobe, an electric toothbrush, and a collapsible iron. My mother folded and unfolded the iron; then she ran it across the snow. 'How marvelous,' she said. 'What do you suppose its purpose is?'

I got the most presents of all, too many to count. The best one was a detective kit with fingerprinting powder and a potion that detected bloodstains. Also a magnifying glass and a roll of police-scene tape.

That night, I searched our house for evidence of a crime. I fingerprinted my parents and looked for bloodstains on the rug. In the living room, I found a dark spot that looked suspicious, but when I ran the test it came out negative. Check in your father's study, my mother said.

On New Year's Eve, Edgar came over to baby-sit. As soon as he arrived, I fingerprinted him. 'Perhaps I should seek legal counsel,' he muttered. Then he went into the bathroom and washed his hands. Later my mother came downstairs wearing her mermaid dress and twirled around for him. 'How do I look?' she asked. 'As lovely as ever, Mrs. Davitt,' he said. The tips of his ears turned bright pink. He excused himself and went into the kitchen to get a glass of milk.

My mother sat down on the couch and put on her shoes. New Year's Eve was my parents' wedding anniversary and they were going to a restaurant in the next town. 'Nine years, Grace,' my mother said. 'That's a nothing sort of number, don't you think?' But when my father came down in his new suit she went to him and got down on bended knee. He laughed and held a hand to her cheek. 'Marry me, Anna,' he said, and she agreed.

Edgar didn't come out of the kitchen until after they'd left. Then he sat in my father's chair reading a book called *The Story of Stupidity*. When I asked him what it was about, he told me it was an autobiography. 'Whose autobiography?' I asked. 'Oh, never mind,' he said.

It was snowing out and the only channel that would come in was the religious one. I watched a show about a Catholic priest who wandered around the world feeding hungry kids. Wherever he went, dirty children clung to him. He patted their heads and wiped their faces clean. My mother had once said that Edgar would make a good priest, but I couldn't see why this was true. He never talked about God to me. Just once, he said he wished he were pure spirit, no body at all.

After the show, I asked Edgar questions about God, but he wouldn't answer most of them. In my notebook, I kept a list of the questions he'd approved. *Does God have a face?* was a good one. *Is God ever bored?* was not.

The next morning, my mother woke me up at dawn. 'I have a surprise for you,' she said. She opened the window and let the cold in. Outside, a few faint stars lingered like moths. My mother pulled the covers off my bed. Her hands were black and smelled of turpentine. I kept my eyes closed when she turned on the lights. 'Rise and shine, little monster,' she said.

I got dressed and followed her down the hall. 'What is it?' I asked her, but she wouldn't say.

'Is it bigger than a bread box?'

My mother frowned. 'Oh yes,' she said. 'Much bigger.'

It was quiet in the house. In the distance, I could hear the rumble of a train passing by. 'All aboard,' my mother said. We came to the spare room, where she kept her sewing things. Now that she'd stopped sewing, she kept it locked up with a key.

My mother pushed open the door. Suddenly it seemed we had stepped outside. The room was completely black. The walls, the doors, even the ceiling had been painted. Everywhere I looked, there were glow-in-the-dark stars.

My mother wiped her hands on her skirt. In one corner was a desk and a small blackboard. On the wall behind them, my mother had painted some words in white. 'It's the cosmic calendar,' she said. 'Everything that's happened

44

since the beginning of time compressed into just one year.'
She pointed to a neatly lettered sign above the doorway.

One billion years of real time = 24 days on the cosmic calendar.
And then on the wall next to it:

THE COSMIC CALENDAR
Jan. 1: Big Bang
May 1: Origin of the Milky Way Galaxy
Sept. 9: Origin of the Solar System
Sept. 14: Formation of the Earth
Sept. 25: Origin of life on Earth
Oct. 2: Formation of the oldest rocks known on Earth
Oct. 9: Date of the oldest fossils known to man
Nov. 1: Invention of sex (by microorganisms)
Dec. 16: First worms
Dec. 19: First fish
Dec. 21: First insects
Dec. 22: First amphibians
Dec. 24: First dinosaurs
Dec. 26: First mammals
Dec. 27: First birds
Dec. 29: First primates
Dec. 30: First hominids
Dec. 31: First humans

On the blackboard, my mother had written: *If one day
equaled the age of the universe, all of recorded history would be no
more than ten seconds.*

I copied this into my green notebook. My mother wiped
the chalk off on her skirt. 'I just thought you should know,'
she said. 'I wasn't sure you did.'

Outside, a car started up. Then a sound like thunder far

away. My mother drew a tiny dot on the board. 'We will start at the very beginning,' she said. 'Then continue on until we reach the end.'

Jan. 1: BIG BANG

In the beginning, the universe was very small. Everything in it fit into a space no bigger than a dot. There were no planets in the beginning. No galaxies or stars. There was only this tiny dot, infinitely dense and hotter than a thousand suns. Then one day a great explosion occurred. The dot burst into a million pieces, streaming into space. These fragments sped through space at incredible speeds. Within minutes, they had traveled many light-years away. They traveled to the edge of what is known, and then beyond. They expanded to fill the emptiness of space, forming galaxies and, slowly, stars. Later came the sun and the planets and our blue home, the Earth. And this became the universe.

I went upstairs and woke my father up. I told him that there was a surprise in the sewing room, but he didn't want to see.

'Let me sleep, Grace,' he mumbled, pulling the covers over his head. Later he came down for breakfast and I showed him the black room. He touched the paint gingerly, but it was already dry. 'Dec. 16: First worms,' he said, running his finger across the line.

My mother came in. 'It's the history of the world,' she told him. 'I used the paint left over from the shed.'

My father cleared his throat. 'The history of the world, you say?'

'I thought I would teach it to Grace in real time. I wrote it out last night while you slept.' She pointed to the dot she had drawn on the board. Beside this, she wrote: *Jan. 1: Big Bang*.

My father murmured something and checked his watch. 'I'm going to the office to do some grading,' he told her. 'If you need me, I'll be in the ninth circle of hell.'

This was what my father said each day before he went to work. For six years now, he had taught chemistry at Windler Academy, but he was always threatening to quit. The boys who went there were made of money, he said. They came to class in cashmere sweaters and busied themselves blowing things up. The year before, one of them had singed off his eyebrows and penciled them in with yellow crayon.

My father kissed me goodbye. 'Listen to your mother,' he said. After he left, she drew a cartoon of him on the board. *I am in the ninth circle of hell*, the caption read.

My mother got an ordinary calendar out of the closet and tacked it up on the wall next to the cosmic one. She flipped through the pages until she reached May, then put an X on the first day of the month. 'Nothing happens in the world until then,' she explained.

I looked at the cosmic calendar. My mother erased the dot that had started everything. Then she opened the door and let the stars fade. We wouldn't be back in the black room for four months, she told me. We had to wait for our galaxy to form.

8

There were only a few other houses on my block, and a blind girl lived in one of them. As soon as the weather got warm, she'd come outside and play on the sidewalk in front of her house. I liked to walk at a distance behind her, matching my footsteps to hers, stopping when she did. Sometimes she paused and moved her cane through the air. Who is it? she'd say. I can hear you walking.

In the afternoons, I hid in the prickly bushes behind her house and spied on her. She had a funny sideways way of walking, like a crab. In the yard, she didn't have to use her cane because she knew where everything was. There was a chair she liked to sit in and a wheelbarrow filled with dirt where flowers grew. Whenever she came into the yard, she would go to the wheelbarrow and smell the flowers one by one. There were five flowers, all red, and she always smelled them left to right, exactly the same way. Then she'd sit in the chair and turn her face to the sun. Sometimes she read a book, using only her fingers to see. I wanted to invite her over to play, but I wasn't sure how she'd get across the street. What if she stopped in the middle when a car was coming and wouldn't get out of the way? What if she fell in a pothole or slipped on a rock? I had an idea that I could put a leash on her and lead her like a dog, but I didn't think she would agree to this.

When spring came, she worked in the garden with her father, planting things. He was small and fat and wore yellow rain boots even though it hardly ever rained. He planted rows and rows of flowers and the blind girl watered them. Here, Becky, he'd say, moving her hands over blossoms and leaves.

I thought the flowers the blind girl imagined must be uglier than the ones I saw, the way you could think of something with wings and see a bat, not a bird. But my mother told me that just the opposite was true. That the pictures in your mind were always more beautiful than what was in the world. Ask Edgar if you don't believe me, she said.

I knew better than that, though. For weeks now, Edgar had been in a horrible mood. He didn't want to talk about the blind girl or black holes or even machines. All he wanted to do was sit in a chair and read. If I asked him anything, even what his book was about, he just closed his eyes until I went away.

But one day I noticed something odd about Edgar. He answered every question my mother ever asked. He told her his height (6′7″), his middle name (Malcolm), and his IQ (160). He told her that he had failed his driving test, that he had never had a girlfriend, that he had once accidentally killed a gerbil left in his care. He told her that he didn't believe in God but that he suspected the universe might be intelligently ordered because of the many beautiful and complex varieties of mold. One day, when my mother offered him a glass of Tang, he told her his recurring dream that he was an astronaut hurtling through space in a VW Bug.

'Oh dear,' my mother said when he told her this. 'I think you may be suffering from a lack of fresh air.'

Edgar put his head in his hands. He was suffering from nothingness, he explained.

My mother went to the refrigerator and took out a box. She poured Edgar a glass of milk and tucked a napkin under his chin.

'Are you aware,' she said, 'that at the end of his life Jean-Paul Sartre renounced existentialism and turned to pie?'

Edgar looked at my mother through his half-empty glass. 'What do you mean?' he asked.

'Just what I said, of course.' She smiled at him and served us pie. It was cherry-rhubarb with crumbs on top. My mother held a forkful to her mouth. 'Heaven,' she said.

We ate until we couldn't move. Edgar had a whipped-cream mustache when he was done, but no one said anything. He was talking about a movie he'd seen in which a man changed into a robot at the end. Edgar felt that this was a happy ending, but my mother disagreed. He told her about a place in the Nevada desert where huge machines fought each other to death once a year. He said that he would go there if he ever learned to drive.

'How fascinating,' my mother said. 'Now, that is something I would like to see.'

Edgar retrieved a crumpled flyer from his pocket. On the front was a picture of a blue giant and the words 'The Burning Man!' My mother folded the flyer into a tiny square. Then she slid it behind the picture of Michael on the honey farm.

Edgar got up and washed his hands with the black soap. 'Always a pleasure, Mrs. Davitt,' he said. My mother gathered up our dirty dishes and put them in the sink.

She asked Edgar if he would like to go for a walk in the woods with us the next day. I was sure he would say no because he hated the outdoors, but instead he said yes, he'd like that very much.

The next morning, he came over very early, dressed for a safari. He wore heavy boots that he had borrowed from his father and an odd sort of hat that my mother identified as a pith helmet. He had on a green vest, with all sorts of pockets to carry different things.

My mother laughed when she saw him. She was wearing jeans and a T-shirt with 'I left my heart in San Francisco' printed across the front. She made Edgar carry our lunch in his big pockets, three Marshmallow Fluff sandwiches and a thermos of lemonade.

I went to the kitchen and got out the bug spray. I wasn't allowed to go outside unless I put it on, not even for a little bit. Sophie had died of a bug bite and because of this my mother had a horror of insects, even the flies that buzzed against the screen door in the summer. If one came in the room, she froze as if it were a bee.

After my mother sprayed me, it was Edgar's turn. He bit his lip as if in pain. She sprayed his arms and legs, then rubbed some on his face.

'All set, then?' she asked.

'All set.' Edgar looked at his hands, which were coated with film. I could tell he was thinking of his black soap, but he just shoved them in his pockets without a word.

'C'mon, my little chickadees!' my mother called. Edgar loped along beside her. His hat was too big and kept slipping down over his eyes. 'Last night I dreamed I was a beaver,' he said. 'What do you think that means?'

I looked at the back of Edgar's head. I had a suspicion

that this might not be the real Edgar at all, but rather an impostor that looked exactly like him. I had read about such things in *The Encyclopedia of the Unexplained*, which told the strange story of William X, who believed his wife had been replaced with a look-alike. The impostor looked like his wife, acted like her, knew all her secrets, yet she wasn't her. She was slightly shorter, she wore her hair differently, and she was much kinder to the children, he said. They lived together as man and wife for several months, until one day he could bear the deception no longer. That night, while she was fast asleep, he dragged her from the house and into the street. He beat her until she was black-and-blue, but she said only that she loved him, that she was his lawful wife. The next day, he went into town and told everyone that she was a witch. He said that she left him at night to dance naked with the devil in the woods. He said that she had cast a charm on his children and turned his real wife into a mouse. In his pocket, he carried the tiny bewitched creature who was his true love.

There was a trial and the man's wife was convicted of witchcraft and sentenced to death. All the townspeople came to see her burned at the stake. William X asked to light the fire and was given a torch. But at the very last moment a white plume of smoke rose from the condemned woman's head. The impostor vanished and his real wife appeared again. 'Save me,' she cried as the flames leapt around her. William X dove into the fire, but it was too late. Husband, wife, and mouse all burned to death.

I kept an eye on Edgar as we walked, wondering if he was a look-alike too. I made a list in my head of the evidence so far. *Edgar or Impostor?* I titled it. This new Edgar answered my mother's questions, every one. He had dirty hands and liked to go outside. The real Edgar had once told me, Nature is a bore. But this Edgar took careful note of all the plants and birds we passed. My mother pointed out the pitcher plant that captures insects in its teeth and the whisky jay that flies as if it's drunk. 'How fascinating,' the impostor said.

We stopped in a clearing and ate our lunch. Edgar wrote down on a little pad every bird we saw. There were blackbirds and yellow warblers and a goshawk carrying something back to its nest. Every one of them I had seen before.

My mother pointed to a whisky jay on the far branch of a tree. 'They mate for life, you know,' she said. 'It's terrible luck to kill one.' She gathered up our sandwich things and put them in a bag. 'Let me carry that for you,' Edgar said.

When we got back to the house, my mother gave him a book called *Birds of the World* that she had already promised to give to me.

I slammed the door and went outside. From the porch, I could hear my mother talking to Edgar about all the different birds she'd seen. At first, it seemed she was speaking a language I didn't know, but after a while the names came back to me: tree creepers, wood warblers, kingfishers, bee-eaters, white-eyes, bulbuls, motmots, waxwings, and something called the bird of paradise.

I climbed a tree and spied on them through the kitchen window. My mother was trying on dresses for the impostor one after another. Each time she appeared in a new one, he clapped his hands. I decided that I would build a trap to keep him in until I could prove he wasn't the real Edgar at all.

I picked a spot beside the garden and began to dig, using

an old ice-cream scoop I kept in the shed. I dug until my arms grew sore and the sun began to set. Then I covered over the holes with branches and waited for Edgar to come outside.

Later, after I had waited a long time, my mother wandered into the garden wearing a long dress. I hid behind a blueberry bush and watched her arranging smooth stones around the edge of a plot. She was singing the song I liked about the boa constrictor. 'Oh me, it's up to my knee. Oh my, it's up to my thigh,' she sang. I held my breath as she moved a little closer to the pit. It was almost dusk. My mother put down four stones in the shape of an X, then wiped her hands on her skirt. I moved slightly to get a better view. She was only a few feet from the trap. Above her, the blue jays were making a ruckus in the trees. My mother took a step and stumbled in.

She didn't say anything when she fell. She just stood very still and looked around. The hole only came up to her knees, but she didn't move, trembling a little as if she couldn't get out. In the distance, a car backfired. My mother leapt out of the hole and ran toward the woods. She was still running when she reached the trees, her dress billowing out behind her like a sail.

When she didn't come back, I crept out of my hiding place and refilled the trap with dirt. I gathered up the branches that had covered the hole and hid them behind the shed. A little voice, like the voice of a bird, told me that my mother wouldn't come back until I had put everything back exactly the way it was before she came into the garden.

Carefully, I refilled the hole with dirt, then smoothed

over the ground with my shoes, dragging them back and forth over where the trap had been. I brought back some stones I had moved. Near the trap were some flowers I had trampled and I propped them up with sticks to straighten them. Finally, when the last twig was in place, I hid behind the bushes and waited for my mother to return. I waited for a long time, but she didn't come. After a while, I got sleepy and went inside to wash my hands. I wandered through the house, but no one was home. I went into my parents' room and fell asleep on their bed.

I awoke to voices outside the window and went to see who it was. It had grown dark while I slept. My parents were walking back and forth through the garden with lanterns. My father had a stick and was poking the ground with it. They stopped in front of the blueberry bush where I had hidden. There was an X shining on the ground between them. The trap, I thought; then I remembered the stones my mother had left before. My father turned suddenly and held a lantern up to the window, but I slipped behind the curtains just in time.

9

When my mother was a little girl, her father invented a secret language for her. He named it Annic and told her to speak it only to him. The trick to learning the language was simple but still hard to guess. It involved dividing the alphabet in half, so that the first thirteen letters mirrored the second thirteen. In Annic, the top letter became the bottom and the bottom became the top. In my notebook, my mother had written me a decoder key:

	A	B	C	D	E	F	G	H	I	J	K	L	M
=	N	O	P	Q	R	S	T	U	V	W	X	Y	Z

It pleased her that her name in Annic had the same letters as it did in English. *Naan*, she wrote in her notebook. *Naan*. Her father had meant for it to be a written language, but my mother learned to speak it too. Soon she learned how to translate from English to Annic in her head and she threw away her decoder key. It was like doing sums, she told me. As easy as that. It took her father much longer, but after a while he learned to speak it too. Only my grandmother didn't know how. Each night, she ate her dinner in silence while her husband and daughter talked secretly. Finally, after my grandfather told a long story in Annic on Christmas Eve, she threw a glass of eggnog at him. 'Stop that!' she yelled. 'You're driving me insane.' My grandfather wiped the milk from his face. 'Jung'f gung?' he said.

My mother tried to teach me Annic, but I could never learn. She talked too quickly for my decoder key. When she spoke it at the dinner table, my father rolled his eyes. He was never any good at languages, she explained. The way he butchered Swahili could have raised the dead. My father looked out the window when she said this. He grew tired of my mother talking, I could tell. Sometimes she talked and talked through dinner and he never said a single word.

My mother thought I would learn Annic if she spoke enough to me, but after a few months I knew only a few words.

On the board in the black room she wrote:

ZNL 1: BEVTVA BS GUR ZVYXL JNL TNYNKL
Bhe tnynkl vf pnyyrq gur Zvyxl Jnl. Vg vf znqr hc bs qhfg naq tnf naq fbzr gjb uhaqerq ovyyvba fgnef. Gbtrgure, gurl sbez gur fjveyvat cvajurry jr frr va gur fxl. Orgjrra gurfr fgnef yvr zvyrf naq zvyrf bs rzcgl fcnpr. Bhe Fha vf na bofpher fgne; vg yvrf ba gur sne bhgfxvegf bs gur tnynkl naq vf abg hahfhny va nal jnl. Rira gur Zvyxl Jnl, vzzrafr nf vg vf, vf bayl bar bs nobhg bar uhaqerq ovyyvba tnynkvrf va gur pbfzbf. Rnpu tnynkl vf yvxr n terng juveyvat cvyt bs fgnef.

When she finished, she read the words aloud to me. If I closed my eyes, it seemed she was speaking a language from a planet far away. The planet of Annic was purple, I decided, and surrounded by icy rings. Everything there was made of metal and it was always night, never day.

My mother rang the bell she kept on her desk. 'Translate this by tomorrow,' she told me.

I copied what she'd written off the board. It took a long time to get all the words right. My mother grew restless, waiting for me. 'It must be your father's side that slows you down,' she said.

That night, I sat at my desk with my notebook and the decoder key. My mother lay on the floor playing solitaire. She was wearing my father's pajamas and a headband we'd found in the woods. I wasn't allowed to ask her anything. Outside, a dog was howling. 'Dhvrg!' my mother said. I wrote out the decoder key at the top of the page and translated her sentences line by line. I tried not to guess what a word was until every letter was done. But some I could remember because they showed up again and again. *Gur* was 'the,' for example, and *fgne* was 'star.' Finally, I reached the end:

MAY 1: ORIGIN OF THE MILKY WAY GALAXY
Our galaxy is called the Milky Way. It is made up of dust and gas and some two hundred billion stars. Together, they form the swirling pinwheel we see in the sky. Between these stars lie miles and miles of empty space. Our Sun is an obscure star; it lies on the far outskirts of the galaxy and is not unusual in any way. Even the Milky Way, immense as it is, is only one of about one hundred billion galaxies in the cosmos. Each galaxy is like a great whirling city of stars.

'Yes, Grace, that's exactly right,' my mother said.

In the spring, my father coached the track team at school. There were only five boys on the team and they hardly ever won. After practice, he came home smelling of cinder dust and drank a quart of water standing at the sink. Then he took a shower and went to bed.

On weekends, when he was away at meets, my mother and I slept all day and looked through the telescope at night. On clear nights, we took it down to the lake. My mother showed me how to find the Dog Star and the Big Dipper and Orion's Belt. Some of the stars we saw were bright and others were very faint. My mother said that some of the stars we were looking at no longer existed. We were seeing them as they'd appeared many years before. This was because it took light time to travel through space to us. It was as if you took a photograph of yourself and had someone walk all the way to China with it. By the time the person arrived, the picture wouldn't look like you.

At home, my mother drew a star on the blackboard with light streaming out. Then she surrounded it with other stars and crossed out each of them.

'We live in the Milky Way Galaxy,' she told me. 'If I sent a letter to someone who lived in another galaxy, I would write my address like this:'

Anna Davitt
52 Larkspur Lane
Windler
Vermont
United States of America
Earth
Milky Way Galaxy
The Universe

My mother looked at me vaguely. She took an eraser and wiped her address away. 'Our galaxy is so big that it takes light a hundred thousand years to go from one edge to the other,' she said. 'Light travels through space at a speed of 186,282 miles per second.' She picked up the chalk and scribbled a series of equations on the board. By the time her letter reached its destination, my mother would have been dead for thousands of years.

A few weeks later, a letter came for my mother. It was in a blue envelope with no return address. My mother turned it over and held it up to the light. She showed me how there was just a smudge where the postmark should be. It could be from another galaxy, she said, but as soon as she opened the letter, I saw Mrs. Carr's handwriting inside. Twice before, she had sent notes home with me. These notes I did not deliver, but kept in a shoe box under my bed. My mother sat down at the kitchen table and read the note aloud. In it, Mrs. Carr regretted to inform her that I was an incorrigible thief. She told how I had stolen the pennies our class had collected for the Ethiopians. Also a ruler, two finger puppets, thirty-four gold stars, and a box of paper clips. *Despite repeated explanations, Grace seems unable to grasp the concept of private property*, Mrs. Carr wrote. My mother laughed. 'Grace, are you a Communist?' she said.

But that night, when my father came home from work, she asked to speak to him privately. They went upstairs and talked in the bedroom for a long time with the door closed. At first, I could hear them arguing, but when they came out, a decision had been made. There was good news and bad news, my mother said. The bad news was I had to give the pennies back to the Ethiopians. The good news was I didn't have to go to school anymore. In the fall, I'd stay home and my mother would teach me. What would we study, I asked her. And she said the history of the world from beginning to end.

10

All summer, it never rained. My mother piled smooth stones in the backyard and called it a garden. Alec and I turned over the stones one by one, but there was never anything beneath them. My mother said that stones were last things and would be around long after people were gone. Other last things were oceans, metal, and crows. I thought that if I filled a birdbath with seawater and dropped a coin in it, I might glimpse the end of the world. My mother said that this was a sentimental notion. An example of another sentimental notion was my father's idea that cockroaches would outlive us all.

My mother liked the names of these birds: thrush, swallow, nightjar, starling; and not the names of these: duck, swift, hummingbird, puffin. She said that if she ever discovered a new bird she wouldn't tell anyone. She knew a man who had found a bird in Brazil with a tiny purple heart on its breast and he had sold it to an aviary where they piped in monkey calls and the sound of rain.

'Where are these secret birds?' I asked her. 'Show me a secret bird.'

My mother laughed. 'Silly girl,' she said. 'There are no secret birds in America. Someone has seen them all.'

I believed that my mother kept a secret bird in our house, though I could never find it. Alec and I checked in the pantry and under her bed. We opened boxes slowly. Sometimes I expected to find an orange bird that could fit inside a thimble; other times, it seemed that my mother's bird would have webbed feet and lay speckled eggs. Once I thought I heard the chirp of a bird inside the sound of the shower, but when I pulled back the curtain, my mother was empty-handed. Alec and I checked for feathers in the bathtub drain. Nights when I couldn't sleep, my mother turned her hands into birds and made pictures on my wall.

Aunt Fe and Uncle Pete planned to visit for a week, but they ended up staying three. Every morning, my mother made them a picnic lunch and they drove to the lake to swim and sunbathe. When she saw their car coming back at the end of the day, my mother would roll her eyes and pretend to faint. 'How are we ever going to get rid of your parents, Alec?' she asked. 'You can stay, of course, but I've had quite enough of them.'

At the end of the third week, my mother had an idea. She would have a party and invite all the dullest people in town. Alec and I sat at the kitchen table and helped her draw up a list. There was Mrs. Finley, who sold dolls made of cornhusks, and Mr. Gowen, who collected bells. Also a family of amateur cyclists, and the newly elected county clerk. My father added two Civil War enthusiasts and the Latin teacher from his school. I voted to invite Mary, but Alec said she was away all summer at ballerina camp.

The night of the party, Alec and I worked the crowd. I passed around cheese straws while he performed magic tricks. For his finale, Alec tore a card in half, then plucked it whole from behind a cyclist's ear. 'Mysterium fascinans,' the Latin teacher said.

My mother called us into the kitchen. 'It's working like a charm, don't you think?' In the next room, I could hear the county clerk telling my uncle the history of the Windler waterworks. My mother took out a platter of vegetables and dip. 'I want to introduce Aunt Fe to the Civil War buffs,' she said.

After she left, Alec picked up a carving knife and held it to my ribs. 'I know a way to cut someone in half so there's no blood. Want to see?'

'Okay,' I said.

We headed outside, but Aunt Fe saw the knife and took it away.

'Motherfucking mother,' Alec said when we got to the backyard. 'Now I can't do my trick.'

We sat down on the far side of the shed, out of sight of everyone. It was starting to get dark. The sky was the blue of just before night.

Alec took out a cigarette and lit it. 'I guess you could say I'm a nicotine fiend,' he said. He offered me a puff, but it made me cough. He took the cigarette away. 'Sometimes I forget you're still a baby,' he said. He laughed as if he'd made a joke. 'What's that?' he asked, pointing to a shadow in the corner of the yard.

'A doghouse.'

'Whose dog?'

I shrugged. I had wondered about the doghouse too. It was in the backyard when we moved there. It looked just like a real house except that it was dog-sized. The funny thing was that it had a real door that could be locked from outside. Also, there was a tiny peephole cut into the wood so you could look in. It must have been a very bad dog, my mother said.

Alec went over to look at the doghouse. I followed him. He latched and unlatched the lock. 'I know a trick where I can break someone out of a room without ever unlocking the door,' he told me.

I looked at him. His cape had a tear on one side where he'd snagged it on the garden hose. Marvin the Magnificent, he'd written on the collar inside.

'How?' I said.

'Get in and I'll show you.'

'No.'

'Get in,' Alec said. He grabbed my arm and twisted it behind my back.

Someone came into the driveway and opened the car door. Alec dropped my arm and crouched in the shadows behind the doghouse. There was the sound of footsteps and then the door slammed shut again. 'The Iceman cometh,' my father yelled to someone inside.

'I bet they're all drunk as skunks by now,' Alec said. He unlocked the latch to the doghouse and peered inside. I stood a little ways back.

'Get in!' Alec said suddenly, yanking me toward the door by my hair. When I hesitated, he pulled harder. 'I mean it, Grace.'

I crawled into the doghouse on my hands and knees. The floor stank of old food. It was too dark to see anything, but I felt something soft underneath me. A blanket, I thought. The room was smaller than I'd imagined, too small to turn around. I started to back out, but Alec had already latched the lock.

'Let me out,' I yelled. It was hard to breathe in the bad

air. I banged on the wall, but Alec didn't answer. In the pitch black, my hand touched something cold and smooth and I thought it was the skull of a dog. I took a deep breath and tried not to think about the dark. I could hear the wind picking up outside. 'Alec,' I called again. Still, no answer. I closed my eyes. I thought that when I opened them the trick would have happened and I'd find myself outside.

I counted to ten and opened my eyes. Nothing. I could hear my heart beating. I thought this was what my mother meant when she said my father was in the doghouse.

I kicked the door with my foot, but it didn't budge. 'Please, is anyone there?'

'Yes,' he said as if he'd been there all along.

'Let me out, Alec.'

Silence.

'Alec?'

'There's no Alec here.'

'Marvin?' I said.

'Yes.'

'Are you going to let me out?'

'Only if you can answer this riddle.'

My knees hurt from kneeling. I tried to shift positions, but one of my legs had fallen asleep. I remembered a story my mother had told me once about Africa. When a child turned twelve, he was taken to a secret hut deep in the bush, she said. This was the spirit house and for three nights he was left alone there while demons spoke to him in the voices of wild animals. These demons told him that he had been swallowed by a monster and was in the belly of the beast. If he closed his eyes for even one minute, the monster would tear him to pieces, but if he survived until daylight, he would become a new thing.

What sort of thing, I'd asked my mother, and she'd said, 'A perfect one, I suppose.'

The wind died down and it was quiet again. 'Listen carefully,' Alec said.

'I'm no good at riddles.'

Alec ignored me. He began speaking in a strange whispery voice like the voice of an old man.

'Picture a locked room with ten-foot ceilings. Inside, a man has hung himself from the lighting fixture. The windows are closed and sealed shut from within. There is no furniture in the room, not even a single chair. The only thing is a puddle of water on the floor below the dead man. The question is, how did the man hang himself?'

I tried to think. Why wasn't there any furniture in the room, I wondered. This seemed a better riddle to me.

Alec banged on the roof with something hard. 'Time's up,' he said.

'The man was a giant?' I guessed.

Alec battered the roof fiercely. The sound was like a hundred stones falling. 'Wrong,' he said. 'Release denied.'

'Please,' I said. I wanted to cry, but I knew if I did, he would never let me out. No one will find me here, I thought, and I'll starve to death like that old dog.

I curled up in a ball and closed my eyes. I could hear a plane passing overhead and the wind moving through the trees again. Nothing happened for a long time. Then I heard a small scratching at the door.

'Marvin?' I whispered.

'The answer is the man stood on a block of ice. As it

67

melted, the noose tightened until it finally snapped his neck.'

I heard a click as Alec unlatched the door. 'You're free to go,' he said.

I backed out quickly before he could change his mind. Outside, the sky had turned from blue to black. Alec was nowhere to be found. In the distance, I could see my mother walking through the lighted rooms of our house. She was carrying a vase of flowers in her hand.

I found Alec behind the shed, smoking. I hobbled toward him but he didn't look up.

I sat down next to him. 'That was a stupid trick. Now my leg's asleep.'

He shrugged. 'So hop,' he said.

Someone turned the porch light on. 'Alec, Grace, come in!' my mother called. She couldn't see us in the dark. Alec ran down the driveway and into the house, slamming the door behind him. 'There you are,' my mother said. She sat on the back steps and waited for me. There was a glass in her hand that glinted in the light. 'Guess what I am?' I asked, hopping toward her, and she guessed a flamingo, because she always guessed right.

The next morning, my aunt and uncle got up very early and packed the car. Alec convinced them to let him stay one more day. 'I don't mind driving him back,' my mother said. 'There's an old war monument along the route. Also the Museum of Cranberries.' She offered to take everyone on a tour of historical Windler, but Aunt Fe insisted they'd already overstayed.

After Alec's parents left, my mother drove us to the lake. It was an overcast day and hardly anyone was there. As soon as we got to the beach, my mother wandered off to look at birds. Alec and I played a game he had invented the summer before. The game was called New Worlds and it began with us standing apart from each other on distant rocks. Each time we played, it was exactly the same. Alec was the explorer and I was the native girl. The object was for him to reach the rock I was standing on before I finished counting to ten. If I reached ten before he got there, I could capture him and cook him in my cannibal pot.

I closed my eyes and began to count. On eight, I heard him reach my rock.

'I've conquered your country!' he yelled the moment his foot touched down. He whipped off his shirt and waved it like a flag. I had to give him my charm bracelet and my ring and all the money I had. 'Prepare to be civilized,' he said.

Alec leapt across the water to the highest rock of all, then stood there for a long time surveying his land. The sun was setting. 'Canada's on fire,' he said, shading his eyes.

'Give me back my bracelet.'

'What's that? I can't understand your language.' Alec laughed and dangled my bracelet above the water. His hands looked black against the sky.

I picked my way across the rocks toward him. He didn't move until I got within arm's reach. Then he sidestepped me by jumping onto the next rock. He did this every time I got close enough to catch him. Finally, I lunged at him and caught his sleeve. He tried to twist away, but his foot slipped and he fell in.

I watched him go underwater, thinking it was one of his tricks. The day before, he'd told me how the great Houdini had been shackled in chains and tossed in the sea. No one believed he'd escape, but of course he did.

I waited for a long time, but Alec didn't appear. I ran to the shore and found my mother. When I told her what had happened, she dove into the lake with her binoculars still around her neck.

Alec wasn't breathing when she pulled him from the water. She pumped his chest until water came out of his mouth and at last he sputtered out a breath. His hands were clenched into fists, but when he opened them my bracelet wasn't there. My mother wrapped Alec in a towel and carried him to the car. He told her that he'd been trying to reach a bottle floating near the pier. Once my mother had told us a story about a woman who grew so small she could be fitted inside a bottle and sent to sea. Because of this, Alec and I sometimes walked along the shore, looking for bottles floating in on waves.

My mother said that before Alec drowned he was slow, but after he came back he was quick. It was as if her dead father's spirit had touched him in those moments he was gone. Her father could speak twelve languages and curse in more. 'He's the one that looked after you, Alec,' my mother said.

That night, after dinner, my father sat in his red chair smoking a pipe. Alec jumped up on the footrest and pretended it was a rock. I made a sound like the wind. Alec toppled to the floor. For a moment he was a swimmer and then he was still. I rushed to him and breathed into his mouth. I pumped his chest again and again. After a long time, Alec blinked and waved his arms. One hand fluttered through the air, then rested on his heart.

My father put down his pipe. He looked at Alec for a long time. 'Did you see anything?' he asked finally. 'Lights and beckoning figures, I suppose?' Alec shook his head. My

70

mother appeared in the doorway. 'What did you see?' my father said again. Alec stretched his arms out wide. He said that the last thing he saw was the wings of a great bird closing over his face. He looked at my mother, lovely in the doorway.

11

The last night of summer, it was too hot to sleep. Only my father could. He could sleep through anything, my mother claimed. To prove this, she knelt beside his bed and played a kazoo in his ear. 'See?' she said when he snored through 'God Bless America.'

In our nightgowns, we drove to the lake. It was quiet out. Just the trees and the dark night all around. At the edge of the water, my mother took off her clothes and dove in. The mouth of the lake closed over her. I was afraid, but I didn't cry. *Shh*, I heard her say. *Don't say a word*.

It was like that sometimes. Her voice in my head, quiet and blurred like a piece of a dream. *Shh*, she said. *Shh*. The wind moved across the lake. It made a sound like a slap when it hit the waves. *The monster lives here*, I thought. I watched the white balloon of my mother's face bob to the surface. It slept at night like we did, she said.

The water was cool around my ankles. I waded in deeper and deeper until only my head showed. I pretended I was a woman whose head had been cut off and was floating out to sea. My mother had told me about guillotines and about the black-hooded executioner who pulled the string. I let my head drift along the waves, singing a sad little song. *I'm dead, I'm just a head, I'm mean, I'm guillotined*, the song went.

My mother swam over to where I was. 'I thought the

monster got you,' she said. A piece of hair was plastered to her head like a question mark. The moon made her skin gleam. I hooked my arms around her neck and clung to her. The black lake of death, my mother called it when we went there at night.

She swam like a turtle with me on her back. There were just a few stars out. We swam out past the end of the pier, toward the darkness that was Canada. The sky was a dingy gray streaked with white. It looked as if someone had wrung all the color out. I thought of the monster asleep at the bottom of the lake. Was he lonely, I wondered. Did he think he was the only monster in the world?

My mother believed that the monster was a dinosaur left over from another time. Once in a blue moon, she said, a creature everyone thought was extinct was discovered in some remote corner of the world.

This happened once off the coast of Africa when two fishermen caught a strange gray fish. The fish had fierce-looking teeth and fins attached to leg-like stalks. Local fishermen were puzzled until a paleontologist came to town. He identified their catch as a coelacanth, a primitive fish believed extinct for more than thirty million years.

My mother knew a lot of extinction stories, but this was the only one that ended happily.

There have been two great extinctions since the beginning of time, she told me. The first one happened two hundred and forty-five million years ago and wiped out almost every living thing. The second one killed the dinosaurs, but no one knows why.

When would the third extinction begin, I asked, but my mother said it already had and that it wouldn't end until the last human being disappeared from Earth.

In the distance, the lights from the shore flickered and went out. There was a floating dock far out in the lake and this was what we swam toward. I tightened my grip around my mother's neck. She was swimming more slowly than before. I was afraid she might fall asleep and sink.

I tugged on her hair. 'I want to go home,' I said. 'Right now, I want to.' My mother didn't answer. She always said that one day she would swim to Canada and I worried that this was that day. I thought about how Alec had gone underwater and seen a secret bird. I made myself limp and slid off her back. I closed my eyes and tried to drop like a stone to the bottom of the lake. The water grew colder and colder the farther I sank. I pretended I was blind. I pretended I was a fish who could breathe through my skin. I thought that soon I'd touch the bottom of the lake and it would be soft like moss. Then I could push myself back up to the surface and surprise my mother.

Something sharp scraped across my foot. The monster's claw. I opened my mouth to scream and the water rushed in. It tasted of mud and silt and filled up my lungs until there was no air left. I tried to swim to the surface. The water felt like a stone on my chest. *You're going to die, Grace Davitt*, I thought, but it was as if the voice came from somewhere outside me and whispered in my ear. Then I felt my mother's arms around me and suddenly I was pulled out of the water and there was air again, cold and clean. My mother dragged me to the floating dock and hoisted me on top of it. Then she pounded me on the back until water flew out of my mouth in a dark stream. I had swallowed a small leaf and this seemed amazing to me. I picked it up from the dock and held it in my hand.

'Why did you do that?' my mother said. 'What's gotten

into you?' Her face was red and the vein in her forehead was pulsing the way it did when she was mad.

'I fell asleep,' I said. 'I woke up and I was underwater.' My mother turned away. When she was mad, she refused to look at me. If we'd been home, she would have told me to get out of her sight.

My throat hurt from all the water I had swallowed. I tried not to cough and remind her of what I'd done. It was almost light out. The sun was a thin red line in the sky like a piece of thread you could pull.

My mother dropped back into the water and I followed her. I put my arms around her neck again. 'This time, hold tight,' she said.

We started back toward shore. Clouds covered the moon, but I didn't care. I didn't like to look at it anymore because my father had told me it was just a piece of rock in the sky, beautiful but dead. Nothing ever grew there and there was no weather, not even rain. 'Poor moon,' my mother said when I told her what I'd learned.

When we reached the shallow part, my mother set me down. 'If you ever try a stunt like that again, I'll kill you,' she said. I tried to take her hand, but she pulled away. We walked down the beach to the spot where we'd left our things. We looked beside the pier where we'd put them, but they weren't there.

'What in the world?' my mother said. She walked back and forth across the wet sand, looking for our clothes, but they were nowhere to be found. Nightgown thieves, she said.

The sky was the color of cement. I looked out at the lake. I had an idea that birds might have carried our clothes away. We stood there shivering in our underwear. My mother's breasts were bare and in the gray light they looked as if they were made of stone. I was sorry now that I'd agreed to come to the lake. I thought of the monster gliding through the water, eyes wide open in the dark.

There was sand in my underwear. I took it off and threw it into the lake.

My mother laughed. 'Shall we be nudists, then? Is that what you have in mind?' She stripped off her underwear and tossed it in the water too. 'Race you to the car,' she said. As quickly as that, she'd forgotten she was mad at me.

I was out of breath when I reached the car. My mother beat me there. She always beat me at races because she ran as fast as she could and never gave me a head start. 'Catch me if you can,' she'd say just before she streaked ahead. It was the same thing when we played checkers. She bet me a nickel a game and always won. Already, I was six dollars in debt to her. Don't be a poor loser, Grace, she said when I complained.

I climbed in the car. My mother retrieved her purse from where she'd hidden it under the seat. 'At least they didn't take the keys,' she said. The car smelled musty, as if we'd been gone for days. My wet legs stuck to the vinyl and squeaked when I moved. My mother put her driving glasses on. It felt funny, being naked inside the car. I covered myself with a map of Vermont.

'Clothes are the only thing that separates us from animals,' my mother said. 'Clothes and a sense of shame.'

'Why can't animals talk, then?' I asked. My mother frowned. She didn't like it when I interrupted her.

'Bees,' she said. 'Don't forget about bees. They do a special dance to tell each other where the flowers are. Whales, too. They sing songs made of clicks that rhyme like words. These songs tell where the whales come from and where they want to go. Then there was the gorilla who learned to swear in sign language. Stupid toilet face, that gorilla liked to say.'

My mother rolled down the window and stuck her head out like a dog. The yellow bus passed by. It was the first day of school. I wondered if the driver knew I wasn't going this year.

I rolled up the window. The air outside was cold. Even with the windows closed, it crept in through the cracks in the door.

'Your grandfather was a nudist, did you know that?' my mother said. 'There's a picture of him at a ball in New Orleans wearing only a top hat and cane. Emmett Elliot Wingo III. Once he drank champagne from a lady's shoe.'

'Why a shoe?' I asked. My mother waved my question away. She was like Edgar about questions. If you asked one she didn't like, she pretended she hadn't heard.

There were no other cars on the road. My mother drove carefully through town. She used her turn signal every time. She stopped at all the stoplights. Shyly, I examined her body. She had her purse over her lap, but the rest of her was smooth and white. She caught me staring and laughed. 'Whatcha looking at, mister?' she said.

We turned onto our street. Her breasts swung back and forth as she rounded the corner. Mrs. McKenzie was pulling out of her driveway and almost hit us. She turned to wave, then saw my mother driving along with just her glasses on. She dropped her hand and drove past without looking. Once she had complained about the broken-down car we kept in our driveway. 'Stupid toilet face,' my mother said.

My father was cutting up fruit for cereal when we got home. 'Oh, Anna,' he said when we walked through the door. My mother went to the bathroom to wash the sand from her hair. When she came out, she had a towel around her waist but nothing on top. I thought of the Amazons who lived in the jungle and cut off one breast so they could shoot a bow and arrow as well as a man.

My father sighed. 'Where are your clothes?' he said. 'Please tell me you didn't drive home like that?'

My mother took the bowl of cereal from his hand. She smiled and kissed him on the cheek. 'Is that a banana in your pocket, or are you just happy to see me?' she asked.

My father shook his head. He went to the window and pulled down the blinds. 'You have to think about what you're doing, Anna. Anything could have happened. You could have been pulled over. The car could have broken down.'

'Don't be silly,' my mother said, though her car often did. Just the week before, we'd had to have it towed from the other side of town.

I went upstairs and got into bed. I tried to sleep, but I wasn't tired. I sat up and examined the place on my foot where the monster had touched me. There was a red mark on my heel the size of a dime. When I pressed it, it turned white, then slowly back to red again.

I went into my mother's room and got the camera out of her bag. I held my foot up to my face and took a picture. When it came out, I wrote the date on the back and put it in the drawer.

12

Sept. 9: Origin of the Solar System
What became the Sun was once a vast glowing mist that spun freely
in space. For billions of years it swirled through the dark, drawing
dust and rocks and ice to it. As it grew, the gas inside this cloud
condensed and soon its shape began to change. Its edges flattened
and its center bulged. A dark ball of gas burst from its core and into
space. This was the newborn Sun, which scientists call a protostar.
Around it, the cloud of dust and gas it came from continued to spin.
Over time, pieces of rock came together inside and formed larger
globes of liquid rock. As they cooled, they became the planets of our
solar system and the moons that circle them.

When the cosmic calendar started again, my mother took
me down to the football field behind my father's school.
First we put down a red beach ball at the goal line for the
Sun. At the thirty-six-yard line, we left a mustard seed for
Mercury. Next we sorted through a bag of peas to find the
smallest and the largest one. The smallest pea, we placed
sixty-seven yards downfield for Venus. Downfield twenty-
six yards more, we put the larger pea, Earth. My mother
paused on the sidelines, calculating. 'The moon should be
placed nine inches away from Earth,' she said. 'A pinhead
will do.' She gathered up our things and walked to the edge
of the field. With a measuring tape, she marked forty-two

yards farther down. Past the track and into the sand of the high jump. In the middle of the sand, she put a BB shot. And this was Mars. 'Back into the car,' my mother said. She drove up parallel to the football field, lining our car up with the beach–ball Sun. 'Watch the odometer, Grace,' she said. 'In exactly one–fourth of a mile, we'll stop for Jupiter.'

I watched the odometer. It only took a minute to get there. Jupiter was an orange at the edge of woods. We drove another fourth of a mile along the trees. Then my mother got out and left a tangerine for Saturn. A half a mile more to leave a plum for Uranus. Then Neptune, a ping-pong ball, two–thirds of a mile away. When we were two miles from the Sun, we put a mustard seed down by the side of the road. 'Poor Pluto, all alone,' my mother said.

When we got home, we watched the season's debut of my uncle's show. For the finale, the question girl wore a sun costume and spun across the stage. My uncle stood stiffly in the lights, wearing a bow tie. 'Yes?' he said when she appeared.

WHAT WOULD HAPPEN IF THE SUN WENT OUT?
There would be no light or heat. It would always be night. Plants and animals would die and nothing would grow. It would get colder and colder. Ice would cover everything. It is likely that we would freeze to death before we starved. Even as we speak, the Sun is dimming. Already, it is a hundred times less bright than it once was. Still, there is no need to worry. The Sun will continue to shine for five billion years.

The lights came up. The stage filled suddenly with dancers costumed as planets. They spun around and around the question girl. The music swelled. When Jupiter leapt into Neptune's arms, my uncle held up his hand. 'Thank you, that will be all,' he said.

My mother threw a shoe at the TV. 'Thief,' she muttered. She got up and paced around the room. A number appeared at the bottom of the screen: *Questions? Call me at 1-800 SCIENCE*, it said.

My mother went into the kitchen and slammed the door. 'Peter Davitt, please,' I heard her say. I put my ear to the door, but I couldn't make out the words. Later she came out of the kitchen and turned off the TV. 'Of course, he won't admit it,' she said. 'He wouldn't even talk to me.'

'Admit what?' I asked.

My mother picked up her shoe from the floor. 'Don't play dumb with me, Grace.' She called Edgar and asked him to baby-sit for me. 'I'm going to the lake,' she said, 'and I don't want company.'

I waited on the front steps, wondering which Edgar it would be. But when he arrived, I wasn't sure. This Edgar wore his hair slicked back in a tiny ponytail like a girl's. He had on black jeans and a T-shirt that said 'Eat the Rich,' with a knife and fork crossed underneath.

My mother smiled at him. 'I almost didn't recognize you,' she said. 'You look very ominous today.' She touched her hand lightly to his shirt. 'A gift from your father, I presume?'

Edgar blushed. We'd seen him in the marina once, tying up his father's boat. *Capitalist Tool*, it was called.

He stuck his hands in his pockets. 'I ordered it through the mail,' he said.

My mother put on her sweater. 'I'll be back before dark,' she told him. She didn't say anything to me.

As soon as she left, Edgar got out the old picture albums from the den. There was a picture of my mother he liked to look at whenever she left the house. He knew which album it was in but he always looked through them all from start to finish anyway.

The picture had been taken in New Orleans, where my mother had lived when she was a girl. In it, she is throwing beads to a crowd from a rose-covered float. Her eyes are hidden behind a mask which she holds to her face with one hand. Above her hangs a moon made of papier-mâché. There were other people on the float too, but someone had cut out their faces so that only my mother's remained. All that's left is a pale hand behind my mother's head and a banner that says *Mardi Gras Sweetheart, 1968.*

My mother had promised that one day she would take me to New Orleans to see the riverboats and the beautiful parades. Also, the alligators in the bayou and the snakes that dropped from trees. She said one of her earliest memories was of her father killing a water moccasin with an oar. *Agkistrodon piscivorus*, he had called it, and she'd thought he was speaking Annic, but later he told her this was the snake's Latin name.

I showed Edgar a picture of my uncle with a python wrapped around his neck. He'd flown the snake in from a zoo and had it drugged before the show; even asleep, it brought the ratings up.

Edgar shuddered. 'I hate snakes,' he said. He looked at the picture through squinted eyes. 'Is that your father or your uncle?'

'My uncle.'

He nodded. 'I should have known.'

I flipped the pages until I found the picture I liked best. It showed my mother as a little girl, dressed in hat and gloves, playing with a dead duck someone had given her. On the next page was a faded photo of my grandfather as a young man; the light slanting through the curtains made it seem as if smoke was coming from his head. Once my grandparents' house had burned to the ground, but he had rebuilt it to look exactly the same. I liked to think that this was a picture of the day the fire had started. I'd read about spontaneous combustion in *The Encyclopedia of the Unexplained* and knew that people could go up in smoke just like that.

Edgar got tired of looking at the albums. We had reached the section where all the pictures were of me. This was the part I liked best, but it always bored him. 'First tooth, first bike, blah, blah, blah,' he said.

He took out a book from his backpack. *The Futurist Manifesto*, it was called. I stood behind him and read over his shoulder. 'Stop that,' he said. 'Go find something to do.'

I wandered into the kitchen, but there was nothing to eat. Just some ginger ale and an old casserole in the back, growing mold. I called Edgar in to see, but he didn't want to come.

'I specialize in poisonous mold,' he said. 'The kind that climbs up walls and makes it difficult to breathe.' He turned the pages of his book noisily.

I sat on the sofa and picked lint off my socks. Edgar moved his lips a little as he read. Sometimes he let out a laugh like a snort.

'What's a manifesto?' I asked him.

Edgar answered without looking up. 'A declaration of beliefs.'

'Do I have one?'

He laughed. 'No, but your mother might. She probably has a drawer full of them.'

'Does my father?'

Edgar frowned. 'Definitely not,' he said.

Later he read to me from the Futurists' manifesto.

We will glorify war, militarism, the destructive gesture of the anarchist, the beautiful Ideas that kill, the scorn of women, bridges like giant gymnasts stepping over rivers sparkling like diabolical cutlery, large-breasted locomotives, the slippery flight of airplanes whose propellers have flaglike flutterings!

He closed the book. Outside, it was getting dark. I could hear the light footsteps of my mother coming up the walk.

'What do Futurists believe?' I asked him.

'They believe in machines,' Edgar said.

13

SEPT. 14: FORMATION OF THE EARTH
In the beginning, our Earth shone like a star. It was white-hot and consisted of luminous gas. There was no life on the Earth then. No water or land. But as the Earth cooled, a crust formed around its molten core. Further cooling created water, which later became the primeval seas. And it was in these dim waters that life on Earth began.

My mother had a birthday party for the Earth. It was 4.6 billion years old, so no candles, she said. She made a cake and covered it with blue-and-green frosting. I ate the ocean and she ate the land. Afterwards, we watched my uncle talk about kangaroos on TV. When was he coming to visit, I asked. One of these days, my mother said.

That night, my father came home from work and threw his papers on the table.

'Watch out for the frosting,' my mother said.

We'd planned to clean up after the party, but after the cake, we were too sick to move. I felt worse than she did because oceans covered seventy percent of the Earth.

My father moved his papers, which were smeared with blue and green. 'What's all this?' he asked.

My mother explained about the party. 'I ate all five continents,' she said.

He fixed us ginger ale and gave us heartburn tablets to take. 'I still think you had a better day than I did.' He took off his tie and folded it across a chair.

My mother wiped off the table for him. 'What happened?' she said.

'They've started a prayer circle at school. Teachers and students meeting at the picnic tables just outside my office. When I protested, they said it was freedom of expression.'

My father shook his head. He took out *Know Your Constitution!* and flipped to the back of the book. 'I referred them to the chapter on church and state, but they weren't swayed. Faith is a gift we're asked to share, they told me. I'm considering calling the ACLU.'

My mother made a face. She threw the last bit of cake away. 'Still, it's better to believe in something rather than nothing, don't you think?'

My father took off his glasses and blinked in the light. 'Not at all,' he said.

The next morning, my mother called in Edgar to substitute because she hadn't slept well. 'Where does your mother keep her lesson plans?' he asked me as soon as he came in. I wasn't sure what he meant, so I showed him the closet with the books my father had ordered for me. One showed a circle of smiling children holding hands around the globe. *The Great Wide World*, that one was called. Another was titled *The Story of America*, and another, *Amazing Math!* My mother had taken one look at these books and packed them away. Oh, these will never do, she said.

In one corner of the closet was a model of the solar system made out of construction paper and wire. In another, a chart showing how man evolved from apes. There was a record player covered with albums marked 'Music Dept.,' and a jump rope labeled 'P.E.' On the floor was a small bird cage with Barbie and Ken inside, eating plastic food, and this was called 'History.'

Edgar dug out the home-school books my father had bought for me and spread them across the floor. He leafed through them until he saw something he liked, then put a bookmark on the page. One of them marked a picture of the famous balloon that had burst into flames and fallen from the sky. Edgar explained that this was because it was filled with hydrogen instead of helium and showed me the formula for each gas. Later he brought in a dead frog and dissected its soft heart on the kitchen floor. He told me that the blood of insects was yellow and the blood of lobsters blue. That night, he gave me homework from *The Great Wide World*. Write a report about the lives of children in distant lands, the book said. One page, double-spaced.

I looked through the different chapters. There were Turkish kids herding goats and Chinese kids burning money for luck. There were English kids rolling wheels of cheese down a hill and Mexican kids eating cakes shaped like skulls.

None of this interested me in the least. I decided I would write a story about the girls in India who had been raised by wolves. This I had read about in the 'Man or Beast?' chapter of *The Encyclopedia of the Unexplained*. There was a picture of the girls that I had cut out and glued inside my notebook. In it, one of them crouched on all fours, howling at the moon. Her eyes were red and her hands and feet were covered with fur. *Kamala, wolf girl of India*, the caption said.

The book said that the wolf girls had been captured in 1920 by a local priest who saw them in the wild and thought it his Christian duty to humanize them. One day, he went with some other men to the abandoned termite mound where the wolves made their den. As soon as the men began to dig, two wolves ran out of the hole and escaped into the woods. The third, a female, attacked the priest and was shot to death. Inside the den, the men discovered two small girls, approximately two and eight, curled up with a pair of wolf cubs. They killed the cubs and took the girls to the church orphanage, where they tried to teach them to read and write and pray. For months they tried, but it didn't work. The wolf girls were afraid of light and ran on all fours through the hallways. They ate only raw meat and growled at the nuns. The youngest one, Amala, lived for less than a year. Kamala lived longer, but she never learned to speak properly. Even after she learned to walk upright, she only knew wolf words.

About her, I wrote:

No body knew woof words but woofs and so the girl was allways sad in the house where the nuns lived. Her sister was dead and the other woofs too. The nuns said You must speak clearer Jesus will help you. But the woofgirl just stopped talking and played only with a ball a person gave to her that was blue. The End.

I showed my report to Edgar.

'How do you expect to learn anything when you fill your mind with garbage?' he said. He crumpled up my paper and threw it in the trash.

My mother came into the room. She had her bathrobe on and her eyes were red. 'What's garbage?' she asked.

Edgar blushed. 'Perhaps garbage is a bit strong. I just meant . . .'

'Let me see.' My mother picked up the paper and read it. When she finished, she looked right past him as if he wasn't there. 'That will be all, Edgar,' she said.

That night, she came into my room and sat on the edge of my bed. 'There was a gazelle boy too,' she told me. 'He lived in the Sahara and was never caught because he ran so fast.'

'Did he have fur?' I asked.

'No, he was naked and had long black hair.'

And what happened to this boy, I wondered. When he got too old to run?

'The gazelles left him beneath a tree,' my mother said, 'and one day the lions came for him.'

14

SEPT. 25: ORIGIN OF LIFE ON EARTH
When the Earth was new, it was covered with oceans, but nothing
lived in them. Only a few elements, forged in distant stars, filled the
warm water of these primeval seas. Over time, lightning struck the
water and caused these elements to combine. This created amino
acids, the basic chemicals from which proteins are made. Proteins are
the building blocks of DNA, which carries genetic information for
every living thing. It is DNA that allows organisms to make copies
of themselves and so to live.

That life began at all was just a piece of luck, my mother
said. And the luck was that the Earth was exactly the right
distance from the Sun. A little bit closer and all the water
would turn to vapor; a little bit farther and it would turn to
ice. She took out a piece of paper and drew a picture of the
solar system, then erased the planets one by one.

'Why are you doing that?' I asked her.

'Too cold, too cold, too cold, too cold, too cold, too
cold, too hot, too hot,' she said. Finally, there was only the
Earth left. My mother gave me a marker and told me to
color it blue. Afterwards, she tacked the picture to the wall
in the living room. 'Do you see now how it's just chance
that things worked out this way?'

My mother got out her old photo album and turned to

the first page. There was a picture of the Mardi Gras where she'd met Michael, then one of the school they'd gone to in Vermont, and another of the car he'd used to drive away. Next came the raptor center where she'd worked in California, and one of her boarding a bright blue plane. After that, it was all Africa.

My mother flipped through the photographs until she found a blurry one I'd never seen. This was a picture of the day she decided to marry my father, she said. On that day he had helped her get her truck out of the mud. It was the rainy season in Tanzania. She was always getting stuck somewhere, but no one ever stopped to help. In the picture, my father has a stick in his hand to scrape off the mud. My mother has one foot out, as if she could kick the tires free. She's laughing and her hair is in a braid. If it weren't for all that rain, she said, there might never have been me.

OCT. 2: FORMATION OF THE OLDEST ROCKS KNOWN ON EARTH

The oldest-known rocks are crystalline. They were created when a molten lava called magma cooled and solidified. On the parts of the Earth that had no water, these rocks were weathered and worn down by violent storms. Some of them crumbled and were carried off by the wind. They settled in basins and at the bottom of the sea. By studying such rocks, scientists were first able to determine the age of the Earth.

On the windowsill, my mother kept a collection of rocks from around the world. Each one had a story to tell, she explained. One might be a fragment from a meteorite. Another had been walked on by dinosaurs. She took off her wedding ring and laid it beside them. 'Imagine,' she said, 'how the first person who found a diamond inside a rock felt. He must have thought it was put there just for him.'

That night, my mother played a trick on my father. She hid her wedding ring in a drawer and waited to see how long it would take him to spot her bare hand. Six days passed, but he didn't notice. My mother froze her ring in an ice cube and served it to him in a drink. 'Don't you realize I could have choked to death?' he asked her when she fished it out for him.

In Africa, my mother said, there is a city made entirely of diamonds that is known as the City of Death. This is because no one who scales the walls of this city ever returns alive. On the far side of the wall is a diamond palace and beside this palace a smooth clear lake. This lake appears to be water but really it is crystal polished to a shine. Fortune seekers, exhausted from their long climb, dive into this lake and to their death. And that is why the word 'diamond' comes from the Greek word *adamas*, which means un-conquerable.

Later my mother came into my room and sat on the edge of my bed. She was in her old bathrobe and her wedding ring was on again. Diamonds were always dangerous, she told me, because they inspire such greed. In the Sahara, there were once beautiful hills composed entirely of them. One day a king and his army were crossing the desert when they stumbled upon this shining place. The king said, 'If you take, you will regret it, but if you don't take, you will regret it too.' His men scattered across the hills and soon what he said came to pass. Those who took some diamonds regretted not having taken more. Those who took none regretted not having taken at least a few, and those who took many regretted it most of all. They were so weighted down by their bounty that they fell behind the others and died of thirst, my mother said.

A shadow passed over the wall. I looked up and there was my father standing in the doorway, a glass of milk in his hand. 'Don't you think you should let her get some sleep, Anna?' he said.

The next morning, my mother folded back the paper and left it beside his plate. *Buy milk,* the circled words said. This was a variation of the silence game, I knew. My mother knew how to play, but my father didn't. He sighed when he opened the paper and saw the black ink. 'Is this really necessary, my love?' he asked. But nothing he said could make her speak. That afternoon, milk appeared. The kind my mother liked, in the glass bottle with the raised letters on the front. When my father came into the kitchen, she poured him a glass. I watched him drink. One swallow was all it took. When he handed her the empty glass, his mouth was rimmed with milk. My mother wiped his face clean with her hand. There was a clinking sound as the glass touched her wedding ring. 'Cheers, Jonathan,' she said.

OCT. 9: DATE OF THE OLDEST FOSSILS KNOWN TO MAN
The oldest creatures preserved in fossils looked like small mushrooms and were found all over the shallow sea. They were made up of billions of blue-green bacteria living together in layers on the ocean floor. Scientists named them stromatolites, which means stone mattress, because of the way they lay together like sheets on a bed. They first appeared on Earth more than three billion years ago.

My mother drew a mushroom on the board. Then she erased it and drew another one.

'Pay attention, Grace,' she said.

I scuffed my shoes along the floor. Already I was tired of the calendar. We weren't even up to the worms yet, and dinosaurs were months away.

My mother said my homework was to find out how fossils were made, then write it up in a report. As soon as she turned her back, I closed my notebook and put it away. *Who cares about fossils*, I scratched on my desk.

It was hot in the black room. My mother talked on and on about the sea. I could see kids from the neighborhood coming home from school. I didn't remember their numbers anymore, but I still remembered their names. Billy McAllister was It, and everyone else was running away. They ran past the blind girl's flower beds, then around the corner toward the lake.

After a while, Jo Pace passed by on her bike. She had on overalls and her hair was cut short and crooked like a boy's. She pedaled fast, standing up off the seat as she rode. I knew she was headed to the junkyard, where she lived with her father and a hundred broken cars.

In real school, I used to give her half my lunch every day because she was saving up to buy a horse. When she got the horse, she was going to run away to Montana and be a cowboy, she'd told me. In the summer, her father let her sleep outside in a huge tire that had once been part of a trailer truck.

'Grace, are you listening?' my mother said. She closed the window and pulled down the shade.

The stars on the wall started to glow. My mother stretched her arms out wide. She was talking about the universe again. I put my head on my desk and breathed in the wood smell. My pencils clattered to the floor, but I didn't pick them up.

My mother whirled around. 'What's going on?' she said.

I threw my notebook across the room. It landed at her feet with a thump. 'I'm sick of the stupid universe,' I told her.

'The universe is sick of you too,' she said.

15

Abat is not a bird, my mother corrected me. It was
Halloween. I wasn't allowed to trick-or-treat
until we had given away all the candy. If we
left it on the porch, people might take too much, she
said. My mother had painted her shoes leaf-green. I
wished it were snowing outside so that her shoes would
be white again.

I went to the window. Outside, masked children
moved from house to house. My mother was a flower
and I was a bat. Flowers were not last things, but still she
liked them.

Just after dark, the blind girl came to our door dressed as a
fairy princess. Her cane had been covered with sparkles and
turned into a wand. I was afraid she would recognize the
sound of my shoes if I went to get the candy. 'We're out of
candy,' I said.

My mother came into the room, carrying a bowl. 'You
know Becky, don't you?' she asked me. She filled her
jack-o'-lantern with candy. I stood very still in my spy
shoes.

My mother walked the blind girl to the door. I could see
her father waiting outside on the steps in his yellow rain
boots. I remembered a witch I'd seen on TV who wanted

the wing of a bat and the eye of a newt. Wing of a bat, eye of a newt, she'd chanted, sweeping the floor with her magic broom.

I closed my eyes and tilted my arms like wings. I flew toward Becky, knocking her to the floor. 'I'm as blind as a bat,' I told her, giggling.

My mother helped her up and gave her extra candy. She went outside and spoke to the blind girl's father. Then she came back and put all the candy away. She shut the windows and locked the door. When I asked if we could go out yet, she held me upside down until I cried. 'See how bats sleep,' she said.

The next morning, Edgar came over, carrying a stack of flyers. 'I've decided to become a Futurist,' he explained. He stood on the front steps and read aloud to me.

Let's break away from rationality as out of a horrible husk and throw ourselves like pride-spiced fruit into the immense distorted mouth of the wind!

And this:

Oh! maternal ditch, almost to the top with muddy water! Fair factory drainage ditch! I avidly savored your nourishing muck, remembering the holy black breast of my sweet nurse . . . When I got out from under the upturned car – torn, filthy, and stinking – I felt the red-hot iron of joy pass over my heart!

When my mother woke up, I gave her a flyer. She read part of it, then threw it away. 'Those aren't even his own words,' she said. 'Edgar comes from a long line of decadent and overbred people.'

When pressed, she compared him to a Dalmatian she once had who was afraid of vacuum cleaners and teacups. I showed her the picture of a speeding train he had drawn for me.

My mother tacked it to the refrigerator with a piece of tape. 'Edgar needs his driver's license,' she said.

She told him she would hire him as our chauffeur so that he could practice for his test. From then on, he drove us to the lake and the raptor center and the store. On weekends, she took him out to the old highway and he practiced passing imaginary cars. 'Watch out for that truck,' my mother said whenever he drifted across the yellow line.

He was supposed to always drive with an adult, but some days when my mother stayed late at work she let him pick her up.

Edgar drove fast, seventy, eighty, ninety miles per hour, but still we were never on time. This was because of the bumps. If you started listening for them, they never stopped. Some sounded like metal striking metal, but others were dull thuds, the tire crossing something in the road. 'Did you hear that?' he'd ask me as we headed out of town. It didn't matter what I said, because he always asked again. 'Listen,' he'd say, slowing down. 'Did we just hit something?'

Once he asked me on a day when we were already late to pick up my mother because of the rain. I shook my head. No, nothing. Edgar's hands were white on the wheel. I watched the odometer click around. It had been fifteen miles since the last bump. Suddenly Edgar swung the car around. He drove back the way we had come, past the church, over the bridge, right to the edge of town. He pulled over where the bump was and got out of the car. 'Wait here. I'll just be a minute,' he said. Edgar walked down one side of the road and then the other. He crawled over the guardrail and looked into a ditch. When he came back, he was sweating. 'It was nothing,' he said.

That night, we were an hour late to pick up my mother at the raptor center. When we got there, the lights were off and she was standing alone in the parking lot holding a newspaper over her head. The paper was so wet that the ink had bled and run down her face. She got in the car and slammed the door.

'I'm sorry,' Edgar said. 'Something came up.' He didn't say anything about the bumps, so I kept quiet, too. There had been five that day.

'Something always comes up,' my mother said. She turned on the heat as high as it would go, then sat hunched over, shivering. Rain drummed on the roof. My mother shook out her hair like a dog.

Edgar drove carefully through town, stopping at all the lights. When he passed the woods, he tried to point out a whisky jay to her, but she wouldn't look. In the driveway, he touched my mother's wrist. 'See you tomorrow, Mrs. Davitt?' he asked. My mother shook her head. 'Consider yourself fired,' she said.

A few days later, Edgar stopped by to give her a pie he had made. It was sunken on one side and burned on the top. My mother was in the garden when he came around. 'Go away, Edgar,' she told him. 'I don't have time for you or your sorry pie.'

He moped around the driveway until I called him in to see the globe my mother had given me. In the black room, he spun it again and again. 'Africa, Asia, Russia,' he said. We sat at my mother's desk and ate the pie. On the board was a lesson from the week before: *Nov. 1: Invention of sex (by microorganisms)*.

'That was the day that all the trouble started,' Edgar said.

16

'How long? How long?' I asked each night at dinner. My father had promised to build me a dollhouse, but already it had taken longer than he'd said. Every morning, he got up at seven and packed a bag lunch to take to the basement. Then he stayed in his workroom until my mother called for him at six. When I asked why he didn't go to school anymore, my mother said it was because he had told a Catholic boy that God was really a monkey.

My father had been working on the house for a month and during that time I'd come to think of him as a basement beast, dull and thudding, afraid of light, his pockets filled with sawdust. For a while, he indulged me in this, lumbering up the stairs with a roar, twirling me through the air, letting my mother transform him with a kiss. At dinner, he smelled always of the basement damp. 'You beastly man,' my mother cried, because she had once wanted to be an actress. I took to saying this too, pursing my lips and putting one hand on my hip the way I'd seen her do. 'Stop that at once,' my mother said. 'No one likes a coy child.'

I had begun to admire a pink plastic dollhouse at the toy store. It had an elevator and a heart-shaped pool. 'Soon,' my father told me. 'Very soon.' I could hear my mother crying when he came up from the basement at night. The bedspread he had bought for her was covered with orange flowers. In the afternoons, while she slept, my mother pulled the covers up over her head so that one of the flowers covered her face. I was terrified of the flower, but I knew better than to wake my mother. At night, I could hear her walking through the hallway and down the stairs. Sometimes my mother opened or shut the window outside my door. After a while, my father would get up and say, 'Anna, what are you doing? Come back to bed.' Then I would hear the soft swish of her slippers and the door easing shut.

I knew that my mother was listening for the sound of our house settling into sleep. Each night, while we slept, shingles fell off our roof like eyelashes. The spindly trees outside my window leaned into the wind. Still, they branched like fish bones against the sky. Rain fell through the roof and into a pail down the hall. Long before my father had started on the house, he had built me ships out of kits. Ships for all the seven seas, he said. Black Sea, Dead Sea, Red Sea, he sang into a song for me. My father said that once a ship had listed on a windless sea for months and when it crashed ashore it was filled with ghosts. He told me of the creatures, half woman, half bird, whose voices sped like arrows through a sailor's heart. My mother grew restless, listening. 'That's such an old story,' she said. She called me to her, but I wanted to hear about the great eyeless fish that lived in the depths of the Sargasso Sea. 'They might be as big as horses,' my father told me. 'No one has ever gone down that far.'

'Why eyeless?' I asked. 'Isn't there anything to see?' My father shook his head. 'There's no light in water that deep,' he said. 'The fish find their way by vibration alone.' He kissed my mother then, once, twice. I closed my eyes. Before I was born, they had traveled around the world together, and sometimes it seemed that they went away again and forgot me.

One night, while my father worked on the house, my mother let me come into her room and fold clothes with her. We put socks over our hands and turned them into electric eels that slithered across the flowered bed. Mine was black and my mother's was gray. The eels danced through the air; my mother made a clicking sound whenever the black eel came too close. I thought we looked happy in the mirror that hung on the closet door. My mother looked as if she had slept well the night before. The rain had stopped and I knew that the sound she liked best was the sound of the wind in the trees. My mother took the sock off her hand. She wrapped my head in one of her scarves. 'Now you look like me,' she said. 'If only you didn't have your father's nose, we'd be just alike.' She laughed, covering my face with the scarf so that only my eyes showed. 'There,' she said. 'Perfect.'

The next morning, I went into the bathroom and found the shower drain covered with half-dead flies. It was already late for my bath and I was afraid if I went to get my father my mother would come in and see them. When I tried to pick them up with a washcloth, they buzzed fiercely. 'Don't bite me, don't bite me,' I whispered like a charm. I could see their greenish wings and the tiny thread–like hairs on their legs. I picked up my mother's perfume bottle, then heard the bedroom door open. I turned the lock and sprayed perfume all over the flies. My mother tried the door. 'What are you doing, Grace?' she said. 'Open the door, please.' I sprayed more perfume, but a few legs still twitched. 'Grace!' my mother yelled. I took the top off the bottle and emptied it into the tub. The black flies were shiny with perfume. None of them moved. I waited a minute to be sure, then picked them up with a tissue and flushed them away. I hid the empty bottle in the back of the cabinet and washed my hands twice. When I opened the door, my mother's fist was raised to pound on it. 'What have you done in here?' she said. 'Have you been playing with my things?' Suddenly it seemed the room was filled with perfume. My mother yanked open the cabinet. When she found the empty bottle, she shook me until my shoulders hurt. 'I only overslept a little,' she yelled. 'You're old enough to take a bath by yourself.' She let go of me and slammed the door. I could see a bit of her robe had gotten caught in it. I leaned over to touch the pink, but before I could, my mother opened the door and slammed it again.

But that afternoon she came to my room and said, 'Today we are going to see your father by the light of day.' We crept through the hallway and down the stairs. We burst through the basement door. My father looked up, startled. He'd shaved off his beard and his face looked shiny and strange. He had a chair pulled up to a little radio and was listening to a ball game. The dollhouse sat on a table across the room. The wood was unpainted, the windows shutterless; it had no roof or back to it. My mother said, 'What on earth have you been doing down here?'

My father straightened in his chair. 'I was just taking a break,' he said. 'I'm actually much farther along than it looks.' I fingered the small tools lying on the table. Out of the corner of my eye, I saw a bug dart behind the house and hide there. My father smiled at me. 'We wanted to see you by the light of day,' I said.

He turned off the radio. 'Come give me a kiss, Grace,' he said. He held out his hand, but I shied away from him. 'Please,' he said.

My mother laughed. 'Don't tell me your charm is failing you, Jonathan? It's not as easy as all that?' Like a deer, she darted across the room toward him. 'My sweet,' he said and kissed her, but still he smiled at me.

'I thought you should know,' I said, 'that I don't even want that house anymore.'

'Is that so?' my father murmured.

My mother started up the stairs and I followed her. 'Don't look back,' she said, laughing. 'You'll turn to stone. To salt, I think.' I ran to the top of the stairs with her. Below us, I could hear my father moving through his room.

The day I turned eight, my father finished the dollhouse. He bounded up the stairs, holding it. I was in the kitchen with my mother making a cake. The cake had turned out too tall and I had frosting on my face and all over my hands. 'Don't touch, don't touch,' my father said, carrying the house outside.

It was almost perfect. My father set it on the front steps to compare it with its model. I shrieked to see my house so small, to see his hand come through the door and greet me like a friendly dog. The house was the same blue as my house; its windows were shuttered as if against wind. There were ten steps leading to the second floor and a tiny pail in the hallway to catch leaks. When I tipped over the pail, water spilled out and pooled onto the floor. My mother said, 'You've thought of everything, haven't you? Don't you think I know what you're trying to do?'

The only room he'd forgotten was the basement; where

the door for it had been, there was only a wall. I touched the spot where my father's door would be. I thought he might have tricked me with a secret latch, but when I pressed the wall nothing happened.

The dollhouse was rigged so that the lights came on whenever I opened it. Inside, wooden furniture shone beneath the lights. There were rugs and curtains and even a fireplace. My mother said, 'Does it ever turn off? It looks so strange, lit up like that.'

But I liked the house best lit up; the empty plates and chairs, the tiny fireplace, lay as if in wait. Someone has gone away, I would think, or, Someone is about to knock on the door.

All day long, I opened and closed the house. I broke two plates and knocked over the water pail before my mother took it away and put it on a high shelf. 'Don't cry, Grace,' my father said. 'Tomorrow, we'll go to the store and buy you plates the size of pennies.'

My mother went to her room. That night at dinner, she turned to me and said, 'You two are just alike. You'd be better off without me.' She said this quietly, as if we were alone, but we were all three there, having cake.

My father said, 'Don't be ridiculous, Anna. What's the point of ruining everything? Let's all sing "Happy Birthday".'

'It's not my birthday,' my mother said, pushing her plate away. She left the table and got the car keys from the hook by the door. 'Wait,' I said, following her.

Outside, it was snowing. My mother didn't speak to me. She just unlocked the car door and belted me in. My father stood in the doorway, saying something, but I couldn't hear him with the windows closed. As my mother pulled out of the driveway, he ran in his sock feet toward us. I could see his mouth saying my name. He looked funny standing alone in the snow and I turned to watch him as we drove away.

On the road into town, I saw two abandoned cars. One had a door coming off and the other was missing a tire. Whose cars were they, I wondered, but my mother didn't know. Later, when we passed the train station, she pointed to a man getting into a taxi and said, 'I should have married a man like that.' As she drove, she pointed out other men she might have married. There seemed no end to people she could have been happy with. I grew tired of the game and began to sing.

'Quiet,' my mother said. 'No singing in the car.' She put her hand over my mouth.

'Take me home,' I said when she took her hand away. I was thinking of all the things my father might build me next. I thought I would ask him to make me a whole town. He could start with the driveway and the road leading out, then the post office and the train station, the school yard and the railroad tracks. All this I put into a song and sang.

My mother stopped the car. 'We will sit here,' she said, 'until you stop singing.'

I opened the door and got out of the car. My mother stared at me for a moment and then drove off. I stood on the curb and waited for her; then I saw the taxi that the man my mother had wished for had been in. I went up to the window, but there was only the driver inside. I opened the door and got in.

'Well,' the driver said. 'Where do you think you're going?'

I gave him my address. 'There's some money at my house,' I said. 'My father will pay you whatever you want.' I gave him the address again, but this time my voice sounded muffled.

'You're a strange one, aren't you?' he said, but he started the car. The meter clicked on. I already owed him sixty cents. 'Why don't you have a coat on?' he asked, as he pulled away from the curb. I didn't answer. I was thinking of the blue house at home and the click it made as it opened and shut.

The driver stopped and waited for the light. I considered getting out, but I didn't have any money to pay him. I thought of my fish-shaped purse lying under my bed, heavy with quarters. The light turned green. Snow fell. From the back window, I could see my mother's car coming around the corner. It careered across the icy street, then slowed down at the place where I had waited. I saw the car back up and then inch forward and then my mother got out and stood where I had been, her hair filling with snow.

There was no one home when we got there. I took the spare key from under the mat and got my fish purse so I could pay the driver. But when I tried to give him my quarters, he threw up his hands and drove away.

Just after the taxi left, my mother's car pulled up. She parked in the middle of the grass and ran into the house. When she saw me, she cried and said my name again and again as if I was still lost and she was looking for me.

Later my father came home and demanded to know where we had been. He had driven all over town, he said, to the raptor center and the lake and the grocery store, but we were nowhere to be found. I looked at my mother. Her eyes were still red, but she'd combed her hair and put some lipstick on. Tell your father where we've been, she told me. Nowhere special, I said.

17

Dec. 16: First worms
Worms appeared on Earth more than six hundred million years
ago. They were small, soft-bodied creatures that fed on nutrients at
the bottom of the sea. But they were different from anything that
had come before because they had heads with mouths and primitive
brains. Also new were their guts and organs, arteries and veins.
Today there are so many worms in the world that even if every other
substance were to disappear from Earth the shape of our planet
would still be outlined by them.

A soul was like a worm in an apple, my mother told me.
Sometimes you went your whole life without knowing you
had one and then suddenly it appeared. In Africa, the soul has
the same shape as the body but cannot be seen. At night, it
travels through the world while a person dreams. But it returns
to the body the moment a sleeping person is touched.

There was a skeleton on my uncle's show whose name was
Mr. Bones. Mr. Bones had no soul, I knew. He was
scooped out inside like a pumpkin. His bones were yellow-
ish gray and worn smooth in some places. When the
question girl crashed him into the wall, his jaws shook
as if he were laughing.

At birth, a baby has three hundred bones. Adults have

only two hundred and six because some fuse together. The average person has six pounds of skin. Fourteen muscles are required to smile. An eyelash lives one hundred and fifty days, then falls out. The heart beats one hundred thousand times a day. The brain sends messages at two hundred and forty miles per hour. The appendix has no real use. All this my uncle said on TV. But nothing about a worm.

At dinner, I asked my father about the soul. Did it look like a worm, I wanted to know. Did it slither out of you or fly away?

'No such thing, Grace,' he said. My mother rattled her silverware into the sink. In Africa, she told me, people believed that the soul lived on after death as a lizard or an antelope. And the very best souls lived on in the moon.

My father got up and scraped his plate in the trash. 'Remember that man who carried the lizard around in a box?' he asked her. 'This is my brother, he always said.' He laughed and rinsed his dishes in the sink. On his back was a note my mother had pinned there as a joke. *Dec. 17: Invertebrates flourish*, it said.

Dec. 19: First fish

The first fish were jawless and had no true bones. Instead, their skeletons were made of cartilage. Their bodies were covered with bony scales and their heads encased in bony shields. They were awkward swimmers and very small. They lived by sucking slime and nutrients off the ocean floor. It was nearly five hundred million years ago that they first appeared on Earth.

My mother told me that before I was born I had gills like a fish, but at the very last minute they went away. Babies have gills before they are born because they float in the womb like fish in the sea. Once in a blue moon, she said, a child is born whose gills haven't disappeared. Instead, there's a slit on the neck that opens and closes each time he breathes. My mother had known a boy in grade school who looked like this. Tommy Linden was his name, and except for his gills, he was ordinary in every way.

I wanted to see this boy for myself, but my mother didn't know where he might be. We went to the library to look through old phone books, but we couldn't find his name. My mother found an old article about circus sideshows and read it aloud to me. There was one in Kentucky that claimed to have a mermaid, but the picture was too blurry to tell. I don't suppose it's Tommy, my mother said.

The next morning, she brought home a mackerel and cut it open so I could see inside. It smelled bad and the gills were spotted with blood. Many fish would asphyxiate if they didn't swim constantly, my mother told me. They had to keep moving in order to get oxygen through their gills and into their blood. She picked up the fish and looked into its dead eye. The worst nightmare she'd ever had was one in which she swam and swam ceaselessly, she said. That's quite enough of you, she told the fish. Then she threw it in the sink.

DEC. 21: FIRST INSECTS
Insects descended from marine worms and were the first animals to dwell on land. The first to venture out of the sea were scorpions, then spiders, centipedes, and a primitive sort of silverfish. In the beginning, they were wingless, but soon they evolved into many fantastic forms. If you had lived in the Paleozoic Era, you could have seen six-foot millipedes and dragonflies the size of crows. Also, a primitive spider the size of a wolf.

112

My mother wanted to skip the section on insects, but I was interested in them. She read a little bit about centipedes from a book, but when I tried to ask her questions, she put it away. Instead, she told me a story about the day Sophie was born. On that day she was so happy she had written her a letter on a napkin, something about how she looked when she was brand-new, and everything that had happened on her first day in the world. But a nurse had thrown the napkin away while my mother slept and now she couldn't remember the words. Had she written me a letter on a napkin too, I asked her, but she said that that was the sort of thing you only did when you were very young.

I went upstairs and drew a picture of a giant spider. Then I taped it to the window in my room. Outside, it was pitch-black. The boy who lived across the street was at his window too. We stood looking at each other for a long time. He had on a white bandage that completely covered his hand and I wondered if he had a hand underneath it at all. My mother had told me that I couldn't play with him because our street was much too dangerous to cross. My father said it was because the boy's family didn't believe in doctors and if I hurt myself over there I might die before anyone was notified.

That night, the boy flashed me a message in code, turning his lights on and off again. I wasn't sure what he meant, but I knew I should do the same. His lights began to blink on and off faster and faster; one short, two longs, short, long, short, long, then his house went dark. Suddenly I knew he had died. I went into the hall and called 911. I explained that a boy with a bandaged hand had collapsed in front of his window. I said I had seen this while I was driving by. A few minutes later, the sirens started up and headed toward me. They came closer and closer. All the neighborhood dogs started to bark. The ambulance sped through the light and pulled up on the boy's lawn. My parents were on the porch in their bathrobes. 'The boy must have died,' my father said. 'They wouldn't have called an ambulance unless he actually died.' My mother started to cry. 'It could have been Grace,' she told him. 'I bet that boy was playing in the street.' My father looked at his watch. 'It's midnight, my dear,' he said.

18

Dec. 22: First amphibians
Some three hundred and seventy-five million years ago, the first amphibians left the ocean and crawled ashore. They resembled large fish except for the four stilt-like legs that supported them. No doubt they ventured onto land tentatively at first, but soon with increasing confidence in their newly evolved legs and lungs. These ancient amphibians are the ancestors of us all. If they had never left the sea, we might now find scales as beautiful as skin.

My mother said that I was an amphibian, that I got legs from my father and fins from her. And it was true that she couldn't stand to be away from water for long. Every morning she went to the lake to walk, no matter how cold it was. But my father didn't care about the lake at all. He had an idea that we should move to the city. There was no place here for him to work, he said. My mother refused to even discuss it. Instead, she clipped coupons and let the hem down on my pants when they got too short. In her purse, she carried a stack of bills bound together with a rubber band. *Urgent! Last Notice*, they said on the front.

One night, she served cornflakes for dinner. 'Top of the mornin' to you,' my father said when he passed the box around. My mother didn't laugh. She didn't even look at him. The week before, she'd started working full-time at the raptor center. There were scratches on her arms from the birds' claws. She was supposed to wear gloves at work, but sometimes she forgot, and when she came home, her hands were torn to pieces.

I tapped my spoon against the metal bowl. Ding, ding, ding, it said. Outside, it was getting dark. My mother got up to turn on a light. I spun the bowl and struck it again. 'Stop that,' the spoon said. 'Can't you give me some peace?' Surprised, I looked at my mother, but she wasn't looking at me. I hit the bowl, harder this time. The spoon was silent. 'Stop that,' my mother said.

The only thing that made my mother laugh anymore was seeing my uncle on TV. For months now, he'd been getting fatter. Every afternoon, we counted his chins. The first one to spot a new one got a prize. As soon as the show came on, my mother asked: How fat am I? and the answer was: Fat enough to be buried in a piano case!

We hadn't seen my uncle since summer. He was too busy with the show, he said. My mother wrote out recipes on index cards and sent them to him in the mail. Lard tacos with sour cream. Cheese-and-fatback pie. Corn dogs in butter sauce. *To your health!* she wrote on the back of the cards.

At first, we'd hoped the question girl might balloon up too, but she stayed just the same. For the end-of-the-year show, she wore a silver space suit and traveled through time. My uncle looked tired as he stepped into the lights. His chins wobbled a little as he spoke.

Is it possible to travel into the future?
Such travel would require a starship that could move at something near the speed of light. Light travels through space at a speed of

116

186,000 miles a second, but the strange thing is that, as you approach this speed, time slows down. Physicists like to speculate about what would happen to two twins – one an astronaut on a speeding starship, the other left behind on Earth. Suppose that they are just thirty years old when the journey begins. If the astronaut travels to a star ten light-years away, the round trip will take nearly twenty-two years as judged by Earth time. In the meantime, the twin who stays on Earth will grow older. His skin will wrinkle and his hair will gray. But time slows for the twin in space. As he nears the speed of light, the ship's clocks slow down. Soon they are completely out of sync with the clocks back home. Yet time for the astronaut feels no different. A minute seems like a minute and an hour an hour. Only when the ship returns to Earth can the true effects be seen. The astronaut no longer recognizes his brother. The twin who went into space is forty years old, but the one who stayed behind is fifty-two.

The week before Christmas, Aunt Fe called and said that my uncle had run away in the middle of the night. He'd left everything behind and flown to Florida with a writer from the show. When my father heard the news, he went on a diet and dyed his hair brown. 'What causes hiccups?' he asked me. 'How big is the moon?' Once I spotted him in the driveway taking a bow beside a pile of dirty snow.

My father wanted to audition for Mr. Science, but my mother refused to even let him try. The show filmed in New York, five hours away. If he got the job, we'd have to live in the city for a year, maybe two. 'I'd rather live in hell,' my mother said.

The next morning, she woke me up early for school. It was supposed to be Christmas Eve, but we weren't having Christmas this year, she said. Beneath her eyes were dark circles from fighting with my father all night long. We tiptoed through the living room, where he was asleep on the couch, but as soon as we got to the classroom my mother moved all the furniture around. Then she ran her fingernails across the board until she broke all of them. By the time my father stumbled in, she was at her desk, reading to me about Tyrannosaurus Rex. He looked around the room, but there was nothing to see. *Dec. 24: First dinosaurs*, my mother had written on the board. My father held a hand up to his head. 'What was that infernal racket?' he asked her, grimacing.

My mother took out a file and did her nails. 'You must have been dreaming, Jonathan,' she said.

DEC. 26: FIRST MAMMALS

The first true mammals were nothing much to see. Scientists think they were timid shrew-like creatures who fed on insects and fruit and lived high in the trees. They arrived one hundred million years after the first reptiles, in the days when dinosaurs ruled the Earth. But then, quite suddenly, the dinosaurs went extinct. They may have been done in by a giant asteroid or they may have disappeared more slowly; no one knows for sure. What is certain is that a world without dinosaurs allowed the meek mammals to evolve. It took a rat-sized creature cowering in the dark to survive whatever killed the dinosaurs and inherit the Earth.

My mother said that the story of the first mammals proved that the meek really would inherit the Earth. That means your father, she told me. Just like the Bible says.

After dinner, he brought up the Mr. Science tryouts again. 'I look just like him,' he repeated like a charm. Already my mother had thrown two glasses of wine and a plate of spaghetti at him. 'What's the harm in trying?' he asked her, but she walked away.

The next morning, he got up early and left before the sun was up. When my mother realized he was gone, she went upstairs and packed his things. Then she left the suitcases outside in the snow. 'Mr. FUCKING Science,' she wrote on the tags. All day long, she stormed around the house in an old bathrobe, muttering. I hid in my room and read about a monster in Brazil that had the body of an earthworm and the snout of a pig. 'Don't start with me,' my mother said at dinner, though I hadn't said a word.

That night, my mother told me about the hyena men of Africa who have two faces, one in back and one in front. If a hyena man meets a young girl on the road, he shows her his first face, which is handsome and human. In back, he hides his terrible face, which has powerful teeth for crushing bones. Sometimes a girl falls in love with a hyena man, never realizing what he is. She leaves her family and marries him. Then one night the man comes home hungry and shows his true face in the dark. He takes his wife in his arms and tears her to pieces with his sharp teeth. In the morning, he tells her family that hyenas dragged her away in the night. Just down the road, they find her picked-clean bones, but no one suspects him because he has on his beautiful face again.

My mother leaned over and turned off the light. 'Wait,' I said. 'Where does he hide his terrible face?'

My mother touched the nape of her neck. 'He hides it here,' she said.

The next morning, when my father called, my mother handed me the phone. 'Tell him I've got nothing to say,' she told me.

119

I reported this to him.

My father laughed. 'Never mind that,' he said. 'I got the part. I'm Mr. Science now. They want me to start right away.'

I looked out the window. Outside, the trees were filling with snow. Is he coming home? my mother mouthed from the doorway. I shook my head.

'Goddammit,' she screamed and slammed the door.

'What was that?' my father asked.

'Nothing.' I could hear my mother throwing things around in the bedroom. I put my hand over the phone. 'When are you coming back?' I asked.

'Soon, soon,' my father said. 'Until then, talk to your mother for me, will you?'

The phone felt hot against my ear. 'It won't work,' I told him.

My father sighed. 'I have to stay in New York for a little while, but I'll be home before you know it, Grace. Do you think you can hold down the fort for me?'

'Okay,' I said. I hung up and went outside. I tried to imagine living in a city, but I couldn't think how it would be. My mother had told me that in New York everywhere you looked there were skyscrapers instead of sky.

That afternoon, a package came from my father with a hundred-dollar bill inside. *Take care of your mother*, he'd written on the card. Beneath this, there was a telephone number. *Call me day or night, every call is free. Love from your Dad (Mr. Science)*, the note said.

I wrote down the number in my green notebook. 1-800 SCIENCE. This was the same number they put on the screen at the end of every show. I imagined my father sitting in a room with a bright red phone like the

President. And whenever the phone rang, it would be me.

But as soon as my father left, a funny thing happened. It seemed as if he'd never been there at all. My mother moved a cot into my room and we stayed up all night, watching movies on TV.

'It's just the two of us now,' she said. 'We're all alone, my love.'

In the morning, she took the rest of my father's things and put them outside on the curb in garbage bags. Afterwards, I wandered through the house looking for traces of him, but there was nothing left to find. Only some shaving cream in the bathroom and a pair of glasses in the den. 'December 27: First birds,' my mother said.

She put on a record and danced around the room with me. Halfway through the song, she stopped and went to the window. She stood looking out for a long time. 'Come here, Grace,' she said. 'Do you hear someone outside?' Cars sped back and forth through the intersection. The yellow light blinked like a sleepy eye. I stood on a chair and listened. Inside, the traffic's buzz was a faint wailing sound; it faltered, then cut off. 'I think I hear it,' I said. My mother nodded excitedly. 'It catches in the trees, don't you think? Then makes its way over here.' She wiped her hands on the hem of her dress. I pressed my ear to the glass. There was a slight hum in the air. 'It sounds like a song,' I said. I waited for something to fly out of the trees. My mother pulled me off the chair and shut the blinds. 'A song?' she said. 'Why are you always pretending with me?'

19

'There are some animals that have no eyes,' my father said. 'They live deep at the bottom of the ocean where it is always dark. Even if they had eyes, there would be nothing to see.' He walked across the stage and got into a tiny car. The question girl stepped from behind a curtain and got in with him. When they drove, their feet were the wheels. This made everyone laugh. They pulled their car up to a backdrop painted like the bottom of the sea. There were coral reefs and fish with whiskers and yellow fins. In the far corner was the hammer head of a shark. 'Careful,' my father said. He moved a little away from it. The music sputtered on. The question girl stepped into the small circle of light in front of her.

ARE THERE ANY ANIMALS THAT GLOW IN THE DARK?
At the bottom of the sea, there are many luminous fish. They glow with a blue chemical light that helps them find each other in the dark. If you tried to dive down to see them, you would die because they live too deep.

WHAT ELSE?
There are glowworms and fireflies, but their light is much fainter. You can catch them in a jar and look at them if you wish.

'He looks like a salesman,' my mother said when she saw him on TV. I liked to turn the dials and hear his voice coming in louder and louder, but my mother liked the volume very low. The best show was the one where he put on a silver space suit and pretended to walk on the moon. He took big slow steps across the moonscape, then turned to wave at the Earth below. His face was hidden behind a mask. A recording explained that, during all moon landings, one astronaut remained in space orbiting the moon. When this astronaut was on the far side of the moon, he was thirty-five hundred miles from the nearest human being. 'No one had ever been that far away from other people before,' the voice said, 'and no one has ever been since the moon landings ended.' The tape recorder clicked off. My father walked to the edge of the moon in his heavy boots. Behind him, a field of stars sped by. 'This is a good one,' my mother said.

That night, she told me a story about astronauts too. Once, thousands and thousands of years ago, God came to earth disguised as one, she said. His skin was silver and his boots were made of light. He came because all over the world man was starving. The age of ice had come and all the plants and animals were covered with frost. Everything was dying; even the giant cats and reptiles that once ruled the earth had frozen in their tracks. Man too was almost extinct. The few tribes that were left hid in caves, weak with hunger. They lived off melted ice and tiny snow worms. There were fewer than a thousand people left when the astronaut came. These people had survived because they were the strongest and the ones with the most hope. He taught them how to use their hands to make fire and how to plant and cultivate crops. Everywhere he went, he left seeds behind, and in his wake, plants and flowers grew. In this way, agriculture was invented and mankind ceased to be a race of wanderers. This was because men set up camps beside their crops and these camps became villages and these villages cities. And that is how we came to build bridges and towers and roads, my mother said. And that is why we feel homesick when we look at the stars.

That Sunday, my mother took me to church. We drove across town to the one with the neon cross in front. I liked this church because everyone sang songs and talked back to the minister. Sometimes during the service my mother closed her eyes and waved her hands in the air too. This was a secret I was keeping from my father.

At the beginning of the service, the minister asked everyone, Who made the world? and they said in one voice: God made the world.

My father believed that the world was made of dust and ice, I knew. Once he had taken me to a zoo and shown me monkeys who had hands and feet just like mine and carried their babies on their backs. This is where we come from, he said, and once we slept high in the trees and leapt from branch to branch without falling. He told me that the Bible was only one version of a myth people all over the world had told for thousands of years, the story of the first man who walked the Earth and how darkness came to be separated from light.

There was a puppet show at this church and in it was a doomed dog who did not believe in God and was always angry. A cow, a rabbit, and a pig tried in turn to speak to him of Christ's love, but he wouldn't listen. 'I don't believe you,' the angry dog cried. 'There is nothing to believe in but the sun and the sky.' The dog stood alone on the stage and shook his paw at the small children below him. I sat quietly among them, my hands in my lap. Then the cow, the rabbit, and the pig rose up behind the dog, and suddenly he disappeared and there was only the minister's naked hand fluttering among the animals.

'One will be taken and one will be left,' my mother whispered. 'Two will be sleeping in a bed and one will disappear.'

A man came and took the puppet show away. The minister stood at the front of the church with his hands upraised. 'I beseech you, Beloved, to love and serve Him all of your days.' His face was flushed. Behind him, the music began. He touched his dog hand to his heart. 'Beloved,' he said once more.

There was a sound from the back of the church and a man came down the aisle carrying a wooden cross on his back. He was a bent-over black man with green eyes that looked like glass. When he reached the altar, he stood in front of the cross with his arms outstretched. The minister spoke in a low voice. He told how Christ had carried the rough cross up the hill, how he had been fitted with a crown of thorns, how he had been nailed to the wood, one nail pounded into each wrist, another in his feet. Each time he talked about the nails, there was the sound from some-where of a hammer hitting wood. The man on the cross flinched each time he heard this. Dark spots appeared on his wrists and feet. He let out a long cry which seemed to catch in his throat. Then it was over and everyone began to sing about a train.

On the way home, my mother made me promise not to tell my father about the man who had been hammered.

The minister had said that Jesus' father was a carpenter and this worried me because my father liked to build things too. I asked if Jesus' father had had to make his cross. 'Oh no,' my mother said. 'By then, he wasn't a carpenter anymore.'

At the church library, I found a book about saints that was so small it fit in the palm of my hand. In it, I read about St. Anthony, who preached to the fish and the birds and was so holy a donkey knelt before him. *St. Anthony is the patron saint of lost things. He will help you find whatever you have lost, if only you come forward with a believing heart*, the book said. Then there were the saints who ate only bark and dirt, who threw themselves on funeral pyres crying, Praise be to the Lord above, Glory to God in the highest.

I put away the book and took out my homework. *Dec. 29: First primates*, it said at the top. My mother came in and showed me a tape about a gorilla in California who had learned to talk with her hands. Her name was Koko and her favorite word was 'gorilla,' my mother said. Does she think she's a person, I asked. Oh no, my mother said. She fast-forwarded the tape to a scene where Koko was being shown different skeletons, one a bear skeleton, one a dog skeleton, and the last a gorilla's. The woman who showed her the skeleton was her trainer, my mother said, and her name was Penny. In the movie, Koko is asked to point to the gorilla skeleton. Right away she does.

Penny (says and signs): Is the gorilla alive or dead?
Koko (signs): Dead, goodbye.
Penny: How do gorillas feel when they die? Happy, sad, afraid?
Koko: Sleep.
Penny: Where do gorillas go when they die?

Koko: Comfortable hole, bye.
Penny: When do gorillas die?
Koko: Trouble, old.

The screen went black, then the credits appeared. My mother clapped her hands. 'See, she knows all about it,' she said.

20

Dec. 30: First hominids

The first hominids, known as Australopithecines, lived on the African savanna nearly five million years ago. They were small, ape-like creatures who walked upright but had not yet lost the ability to climb trees. Scientists believe they were an evolutionary dead end, but similar hominids arose in their wake. Over time, these primitive humans learned to make tools and conquer fire. They hunted communally and may have communicated with simple signs. Perhaps one of the earliest consequences of their developing consciousness was a dim awareness of their own end.

A sparrow's heart beats four hundred and sixty times a minute. A man's, just seventy-eight. But sometimes, at night, my heart approached sparrow speed. This happened when the darkness crept into my bed and wrapped itself around my feet. It made a low whirring sound when it touched me. Then it crawled onto my chest and lay there, daring me to breathe. If I did, it would kill me, for this was the agreement we had made.

I never knew how long it would stay. Once, it seemed to curl up on my arm and fall asleep. Another time, it brushed across my face and left through the window with a quick rustling sound. This was the sound of all the creatures that waited in the dark, I knew. At night, they roamed the woods behind my house, calling out their names to me.

I was afraid that one night these creatures might come for me. I thought this because of a story I had read in *The Encyclopedia of the Unexplained*. The book said that once in China a creature who was half man and half ape climbed through a window and carried off a girl. This happened very early in the morning when no one else was awake. The creature ran with the girl through the empty streets, dragging her long hair along the ground. She screamed and screamed, but no one heard. But then, just before they reached the woods, some women working in a field saw the beast and chased after him. They rescued the girl and hacked the beast to death with their metal hoes. Some of them took home bits of his hair as souvenirs. The dead beast had hair like a yak, but his hands were smooth like a man's. A young biologist who lived in the town cut off its hands and preserved them in a jar. 'I think he was in love with the girl,' my mother said. The biologist, I thought she meant, but later I wondered if it was the monster.

In the winter, there was an owl that lived in the tree outside my window. The call of an owl meant a baby would die, my mother had told me. In Africa, when this happened, the woman nearest the owl cried, *Ameliliwa*, which meant, 'My baby has been hooted over,' and everyone in the village came to see the baby one last time. Sometimes, after it died, the baby's father went into the woods and shot an owl, but this only brought more bad luck. Had my father done this when Sophie died, I wondered, but my mother wouldn't say.

The darkness moved through my room like smoke. Sometimes I saw it and other times I could see right through it. I never told anyone about the way it moved across me, but one night my mother opened the door and scared it away. When I saw her, I screamed without making a sound. Only my mouth opened.

My mother rushed to my bed. 'What is it?' she asked. 'Did you have a bad dream?' I tried to speak, but no words came. I could feel the darkness in the corner watching me. My mother turned on a lamp. When she did, the darkness slid under my dresser and hid there.

'What were you dreaming?' she asked. She stroked my hair with her cool hands. Now that my father was gone, I sometimes dreamed we were the last two people left on Earth.

I shook my head.

'Tell me what happened,' she said.

There were still a few shadows left in the corner. I closed my eyes. 'My legs wouldn't move,' I told her. 'I woke up and I couldn't breathe.' I shivered a little, thinking of how the dark thing had pinned me down. My mother pressed her hands against my chest.

'Like that?' she asked.

Yes, like that. In the dim light, her face looked strange. For a moment, I thought she might be someone pretending to be my mother and not my real mother at all.

She took my hand. 'This thing that comes is called the Old Hag,' she said. 'All over the world, people speak of it, though they call it by different names.'

'Does it come to you?'

'Sometimes,' she said. 'And when it comes, it brings with it every black and terrible thing. Some have claws and teeth, some wings, but each has a horrible voice that whispers and whispers in the dark.'

I thought of how the voice I heard at night started in my head, then moved to fill every corner of the room. Was it the same as the voice she heard?

My mother squeezed my hand tightly. 'I'll tell you a secret, Grace. All you have to do is say the name of the Old Hag out loud and she will vanish. One brave word and she will disappear.'

This was no help, of course, for how could I speak when I couldn't breathe?

'I can't,' I said.

'Practice with me, then.'

'No,' I said and started to cry. Soon she would go away and leave me in the dark again, I knew.

My mother went to the window. The wind was bending the trees back and forth. On my wall was a map of the world. As I watched, a tree's shadow covered China like the fingers of a hand.

'There is another way to get rid of the Old Hag,' my mother said, 'but it's much worse because it means you must become a black thing too.'

I stopped crying and looked at her. 'What is it?' I said.

My mother knelt beside my bed. 'If you say the Lord's Prayer backwards, then call out "Hag. Good Hag," your enemy will be visited by the Old Hag that night instead of you.'

'But what happens to the enemy?'

'He dies of fright.'

She lay down beside me on the bed. 'I'll stay here until you fall asleep,' she said.

I closed my eyes and tried to sleep. I could hear her breathing and the sound of the clock ticking away. Otherwise, it was quiet. But soon there was the voice again. It began very softly, hiding itself in the noise of the wind. *I'll wait*, it said. *I am quiet but I am here.*

I started to shake. My mother woke up and stilled me. 'What is it?' she said. 'What were you dreaming?' She stroked my hair with her cool hands, but I could feel the darkness burrowing into me. I closed my eyes, but it came in my ears. I covered my ears, but it came in my mouth. Then it went to work sealing my throat. When I gasped for breath, my mother laid her hands on me and started to pray.

Amen, ever and forever glory the and power the and kingdom the is thine for, evil from us deliver but temptation into not us lead. Us against trespass that those forgive we as trespasses our us forgive and bread daily our day this us give. Heaven in is it as earth on done be will thy, come kingdom thy, name thy be hallowed, heaven in art who father our.

Her voice was like water falling. It made me want to sleep. When I closed my eyes, the house of my mother's enemy appeared. Inside it, someone was dancing, following footsteps along the floor. *One two, one two three*, a woman sang. The music stopped and it was quiet again. There was a sound like the beating of a heart. Suddenly the darkness flew through the window and leapt at the dancer's throat. 'Hag. Good Hag,' my mother said.

21

DEC. 31: FIRST HUMANS
Modern humans, known as Homo sapiens, first appeared on Earth
forty thousand years ago. We walk upright, use tools, and live in
complex social groups. We communicate through a shared language
of signs and symbols and spend an extraordinary amount of time
raising our young. Our species invented agriculture, the alphabet,
arithmetic, and art. We are the only animals to have left a deliberate
record of our history and the only ones to have devised a means with
which to end it. On the cosmic calendar, we do not appear until the
last few hours of New Year's Eve.

On the last day of the year, my father came back. His hair
was combed differently and his eyes were blue. He took out
his keys and tried the door, but already my mother had
changed the locks. He stood outside in the snow calling her
name. 'Let me in, Anna,' he said. 'I have something for
you.'

My mother sat in the living room with me, debating
whether to let him in. It was their tenth wedding anniversary. 'He's supposed to give me paper,' she told me.
'What do you think it could be?'

Finally, she undid the dead bolt and opened the door.
My father was wearing a gray suit and holding a bottle of
champagne. He kissed her cheek and handed it to her. My

mother wrinkled her nose and held the bottle at arm's length. 'Is this the gift?' she asked.

My father laughed. 'No, no, no.' He blindfolded my mother and led her down the street. She kept tilting her head back so she could still see. 'This better be good, Jonathan,' she told him.

When we reached the end of the street, my father stopped in front of a big purple car. Purple was my favorite color, and my mother's too. He took off her blindfold and handed her some keys. 'I put it in your name, Anna,' he said.

My mother walked all the way around the car, kicking the tires. Then she got in and sat behind the wheel.

My father stood on the curb, waiting nervously. 'There's air-conditioning,' he told her. 'Power steering too.'

Finally, my mother got out of the car and kissed him on the cheek. 'You're supposed to give me paper, silly,' she said.

That night, he took her to dinner at the Flaming Sword. This was my mother's favorite restaurant because every dish on the menu was set on fire as it was served.

Edgar came over to baby-sit and sat glumly in the kitchen, drinking chocolate milk. 'I can't believe she took him back,' he said.

But just before ten, my mother came home alone. Her lipstick was smeared and her coat was wet where she'd dragged it through the snow. 'Your father's running off to Brazil for two months,' she said. 'Some stupid special about the rain forest, he claims.'

She threw her wet coat on the floor. Edgar picked it up and smoothed the wrinkles out. Where was Mr. Davitt now, he asked.

My mother shrugged. 'Halfway to the Amazon, I hope.'
She took out the champagne and poured herself a glass.
'Would you like a little, Edgar?' she asked.

He straightened up in his chair. 'Yes, please, Mrs. Davitt,'
he said.

My mother went into the living room and put a record
on. She looked out the window and sipped her drink.
Edgar drank his champagne quickly, then poured himself
another glass. My mother came back in the kitchen and sat
down across from him. Every time her glass got low, he
filled it up again. 'Whoa there, cowboy,' she said, covering
it with her hand.

She went into the hall closet and took down a box. 'Do
you know how to play backgammon, Edgar?' she asked.

He shook his head. 'I'm not much for games, Mrs.
Davitt, you know.'

My mother opened the board and set it up on the table.
'Don't worry. I'll show you,' she said.

They started to play. Edgar kept stopping to read the
rules. 'I'll tell you if you're cheating,' my mother insisted,
but he checked them anyway.

I put on my coat and went outside to look at the new car.
My mother had parked it under the streetlight and it
gleamed in the dark. The Purple Pig, she'd named it. After
my father, she said. I imagined him trekking through Brazil,
where the monster who was half pig and half worm lived.
What would he do if he saw it, I wondered. Would he
bring it back alive?

I lay down in the snow and looked at the sky. It was
a clear night and all the stars were out. Too many to
count. I could feel the cold seeping in through my coat
and wrapping itself around me. I closed my eyes and

pretended I was a cave girl who lived in the Ice Age.

My mother came out on the steps and called for me. Her voice sounded odd, like a record slowed down. She stood on the porch, holding her drink. 'I'm not kidding, Grace,' she said, then turned and closed the door.

When I came in, Edgar was wearing my father's fur hat and dancing around the room. The backgammon board had fallen off the table and the pieces were scattered all over the floor. 'Did you know Edgar's half Russian?' my mother asked.

He took her hands and spun her around. On the record, a man yelled, 'Aye! Aye! Aye!'

'Can you speak Russian?' my mother asked.

Edgar shook his head.

'I can,' she said. She collapsed on the couch and winked at me.

Edgar sat beside her with the hat in his hand. 'Say something, Mrs. Davitt,' he told her. 'Anything at all.'

My mother leaned forward and touched his knee. 'Pnyy zr Naan,' she said, then fell fast asleep.

22

To celebrate the end of the cosmic calendar, my mother proposed a trip to New Orleans. She had lived there as a girl and it was the only city she ever loved, I knew. My grandfather was buried in New Orleans, and when we went there we would visit his grave, she said. Also, we would ride on a riverboat and watch the parades. What else was there to see, I asked her. Sunshine and zombies, my mother said.

I thought the trip to New Orleans was another of my mother's passing plans, like the one to become a beekeeper or learn Tai Chi, but that night she stayed up until dawn and packed our car full of things. She packed the monster photographs and the dishes and the badminton net. Also, the complete set of encyclopedias and her wedding dress. In the box she gave me, I packed my detective kit and my globe and the ice-cream scoop for digging holes. Good thinking, Grace, my mother said.

There had been a snowstorm the night before and the driveway was slick and wet. I stumbled a little on the walk, handing my mother things. She chattered happily to me, slipping back and forth across the ice. She had bought some rope to tie the trunk of our car shut and we struggled with this, looping it through the luggage rack. Already, the Purple Pig was filled with boxes. Wait here, my mother told me. She went inside and returned with her bathing suit and the fondue pot. When were we coming back, I asked her. Oh, you never know, she said.

Early the next morning, we went to the bank. My mother retrieved my father's credit cards from the safe-deposit box. There were three of them fastened together with a rubber band. *Use only in the event of an emergency*, the note on top said.

We stopped at the general store and bought snakebite kits and fifty cans of mosquito spray. My mother was talking so quickly that at first the clerk couldn't follow what she said. 'There's no time to waste,' she told him. 'We must be off today.'

When we got home, my mother pulled the curtains closed and shut the door to every room. She locked up the shed and unplugged the phone. Did my father know where we were going, I asked her. Of course, of course, she said. She helped me carry my suitcase and sleeping bag outside. The car was so full that I had to keep them in the front under my feet.

We went inside and waited for Edgar, who had promised to look after the house. When he arrived, he had a present for my mother wrapped in tinfoil. 'A present!' she said. She opened it and inside was a book called *Your Dreams Interpreted*. The book had been published in 1907 and had listings for carriage and cavalry but not for car. 'How marvelous,' my mother cried. 'I'll consult it every day.'

She hugged Edgar and smoothed out the collar of his shirt. 'Well, we're off, then,' she said. 'Remember, not a word to anyone until we return.'

Edgar nodded gravely. He blinked his eyes like he might

cry. Just before he came over, I'd asked my mother if he could come with us, but she said we could never afford to keep him in soap.

It was snowing steadily as we made our way down the slippery walk. 'Soon we'll be in sunny New Orleans,' my mother said. Edgar stood on the front porch without his coat on, waving goodbye. As soon as we pulled out of the driveway, he put his hand to his head and went inside. 'Poor boy,' my mother said.

When we got to the end of the block, my mother remembered the photo albums in the cabinet under the TV. 'I knew we'd forgotten something. Just you run in and get them, Grace.' As I started to get out of the car, she caught my arm and said, 'Sneak in, so Edgar won't see you. We don't want to say goodbye all over again.' She handed me her set of keys. 'Quickly now,' she told me.

I ran through the snow to the back of the house and let myself in through the side door. I could see Edgar in the kitchen, but he didn't see me. I snuck into the living room and got the photo albums out. One was missing, I noticed. I looked in the other drawers but it wasn't there. I tiptoed down the hallway and looked through the open door. Edgar was sitting at the kitchen table surrounded by dirty dishes my mother had left behind. On the chair beside him was the photo album I was looking for. Edgar picked up a glass smeared with my mother's lipstick. He turned it around in his hand, then matched his mouth to the print.

When I got back to the car, my mother was revving the engine. 'What took you so long?' she asked. I threw the photo albums in the back seat and she took off down the road like a woman chased. As we passed the old pier, she took a picture of the frozen lake. 'Goodbye, monster,' she said. She didn't slow down again until we crossed the state line. 'We're home free now, Grace,' she told me as we left Vermont behind.

On our second day, my mother left her purse on top of the car at a rest stop. By the time she realized what she'd done, we'd been driving for miles. I started to cry. 'Don't start with me, Grace,' my mother said. She turned around and drove back the way we'd come. She drove so fast the trees began to blur, and I was happy, thinking we were headed home.

We came around a bend in the road and there was the purse, spilled out into a ditch just past where we stopped. All the money was there. The credit cards too. Only her lipstick was broken, and even that, my mother said, could be fixed. We stopped at a hamburger stand to celebrate. My mother paid for everything with the unstolen money. Afterwards, she made a show of putting her purse in the car. 'Only good luck from now on,' she said.

We saw an odd thing along the way, a restaurant that had burned down except for one booth. We climbed over the burned tables and had a picnic there, but when I bit into my sandwich it tasted like smoke. Where's your spirit of adventure, Grace, my mother said when I complained.

As we drove, my mother described what we would have seen if we had traveled through North America fifteen thousand years ago. Glaciers would have covered most of what is now New England and Canada, she said. There would be huge spruce forests and vast lakes across much of the Great Plains. Enormous expanses of juniper, pinyon, and oak would cover the Southwest. There would be woolly mammoths roaming the plains, as well as mastodon, camels, and four-horned antelope. In the Grand Canyon, there would be mountain goats, and on the great flats of Utah, musk oxen. If we traveled back in time, we'd see beavers the size of black bears, rodents the size of sheep-dogs, and, in the Southwest, large lumbering sloths the size of giraffes. To hunt them, there would be lions, cheetahs, and two kinds of saber-toothed cats. 'Just think, all this in America,' my mother said.

We drove and drove, stopping only to eat. My mother didn't seem to need to sleep at all. She talked excitedly about all manner of things. She told me about a tribe in Africa where the women married stones instead of men. She told me that the day before Michael disappeared he'd had a blue target tattooed on his chest. She told me her grandmother had had six toes on each foot and because of this wore shoes even at the beach. Whenever I pointed out motels to her, she said, 'Let's just go on a little farther, Grace,' and so I dozed in my seat, waking suddenly to the lights of cars and the sound of my mother's soft voice in the dark. On the endless back roads of the South, she taught me how to say my name again and again until it unhinged itself from me and disappeared into the night.

In Georgia, we fought beneath the light of a giant peach. I wanted to have our picture taken, but my mother liked to pretend we were invisible wherever we went.

Later I saw a dark cloud skimming across the sky like a dragonfly and it seemed strange to think that my father was looking at a different sky or not at all. When my mother stopped for gas, a piece of paper fell out of her purse and dropped on the ground. I picked it up and put it in my notebook. When we finally stopped to sleep, I took it out and read it again. *You get money when you need it*, the note said.

I often found notes like this that my mother had written, and it was like finding a bottle with a piece of paper inside. That night, she told me the old story again about the woman who had been left behind on a desert island by the man she loved. She waited for him to return for many years, surviving on seaweed and sand, until at last she grew so small she could fit herself inside a bottle and roll into the sea. Who found the bottle, I wondered, but my mother said no one knew what had happened to it or where the woman had wanted to go. A fish could have swallowed the bottle, she said, or it could have been dashed against rocks. Other possibilities: sharks, mermaids, lonely sailors at sea.

23

In New Orleans, there is always a parade, my mother said. The day we arrived, we came across one outside the farmer's market. A woman dressed as a tomato danced with a green-bean man. Roving vegetables smashed pumpkins in the street. There was wheat in everyone's hair. Two drunken carrots trailed the parade, holding each other up. The woman's lipstick was smeared. Her stalk of a hat was half off. She was a pretty blonde, but tired-looking. She wore white heels and an anklet that caught the sun. The carrot spun her into his arms. Her hat flew off. She slipped on the pumpkins in the street. He pulled her up and kissed her. A float passed by, filled with beautiful maidens, waving from a palace of corn. As it turned onto the main street, a huge pillar of corn fell off and rolled into the gutter. My mother rushed out to get it. Later she tied it to the top of the car and we drove around until it got dark. 'We'll start a new religion,' my mother said. 'People will come from miles around to see our miraculous corn.'

That night, she read aloud to me from the book of dreams. *There is no better dream than to dream of corn*, the book said.

We rented a furnished apartment in the Garden District for fifty dollars a week. There were leaks in the ceiling and mice in the walls, but still we liked it because of the balcony overlooking the street. My mother put the miraculous corn in the window so that people could see it as they passed by. Someone might knock on our door and ask to touch it, she explained. My mother slept lightly with her shoes on just in case, but no one ever did.

One morning, we got up very early and went to the cemetery where my grandfather was buried. I was curious to see this place because he had died in his sleep just three weeks before I was born. 'Oh, Papa would have liked you,' my mother said. 'He never liked your father, but he would have liked you.' My grandfather studied metaphors, she explained. He wanted to know why the brain compares things. Whenever they'd go for drives, he'd make up songs for my mother along the way. The road is a ribbon, he sang. The moon is a pie. My father was a long walk in tight shoes, he told her the night before he died.

When we got to the cemetery, the sky was still gray. My mother parked on a side street and lifted me over the locked gate. I went around to the front and let her in. We wandered in and out of the little grass paths, looking for Emmett Elliot Wingo III. We looked all over the cemetery but we couldn't find his name. Someone must have moved him, my mother said. She took out a handkerchief and held it to her face. The graves were odd-looking, like little houses raised off the ground. This was because the city was below sea level, my mother explained. If the graves were in the ground, a flood might come and wash the dead people away. We passed a stone tomb with small bottles and dishes of food laid out on its ledge. These were gifts for the lwas, who were the spirits of the dead. They liked food and liquor just like real people, my mother told me. At night, the voodoo priests came to the cemetery and left offerings for them.

Some nights we lay in the tall grass of the abandoned lot across the street and pretended we were in the country. My mother pointed out constellations through the haze of heat. The rough grass scratched our arms and legs. We had to squint to miss the streetlights and the chicken place on the corner. From the sidewalk, there were voices. A few feet away, a man passed, singing. He stopped and threw up in the street. Across from us was a crumbling brick building. An orphanage, the neighbors said, but there were never any kids around. Just pink flyers in the street each morning that said, 'Pregnant? Alone? Who can you turn to?'

The man who lived next door to us was named Mr. Candeau and worked as a professional positive thinker, he said. This meant he traveled around the city lecturing kids about how important it was to stay in school. The day we moved into the building, he gave me a blinking button that said, 'I am the future!' which I kept in a box under my bed. Mr. Candon't, my mother called him, but not to his face.

One day, when we slept through flooding rains, Mr. Candeau banged on the door to tell us to move our car. To do this, we had to cross the river of our street. We went out barefoot. In moments, we were drenched, the dark water up to my waist. My mother picked me up and carried me across the street, laughing. The sidewalk was full of people. Everyone rushed around, water streaming down their faces. The chicken place on the corner had been appointed an island and clumps of people huddled beneath the smiling chicken sign. By the time we made it to the car, the water was up to the door handles. My mother bailed it out with a coffee cup and discussed the possibility of electrocution. We decided to risk it. She turned the key and the good car started. We half drove, half floated away in search of higher ground. Along the river, the wind lashed the green trees back and forth in the rain. Lightning cut the sky. Cars filled every possible lot. My mother kept driving, her bare feet underwater. 'How happy are we?' she asked me, and the answer was, Happy as clams.

But the next day the car mildewed and stank of river water. The phone was cut off because my mother had stayed up all night calling Africa. Not to worry, my love, she told me. Money could be found. The phone would come back on. Someday we would drive our sweet-smelling car home, saying, We always thought of you. You never for a moment left our hearts.

There was a bar down the road from us called the Bitter End where my mother liked to go. We went there after dinner almost every night because the bartender let me play the jukebox for free. Sometimes he danced with my mother when a sad song came on. His name was Wink, she said. Just like an eye. He told us how he had come to New Orleans for Mardi Gras when he was just sixteen and never left again. Everywhere we went in the city, people told us this same thing. I came here ten years ago for one Mardi Gras, said the waitress, the cab driver, the hot-dog man. And just look at me now.

I liked to sit at the counter and watch Wink tending bar. He never stopped smiling and he talked almost as fast as my mother did about all sorts of different things. 'Your highness,' he always called me, as in 'Would your highness care for a soda pop today?'

Behind the bar were pickled eggs in a red jar that looked like medicine. My mother ate them with a dash of salt for dinner and claimed they were her favorite thing. I always asked if I could try one, but she told me they weren't for kids. Wink brought me a bowl of peanuts instead. That Wink, my mother said.

The only bad thing about New Orleans was the heat. At night, we filled bath towels with ice cubes and held them to our wrists. When it was too hot to sleep, my mother read to me for hours from the natural history of St. Hildegard. About birds, St. Hildegard wrote:

Birds are colder than animals that live on the earth, because they are not conceived in such intense and heated desire. Just as birds are lifted up into the air by their feathers and can remain wherever they wish, the soul in the body is elevated by thought and spreads its wings everywhere.

My mother decided to take me to the zoo. The world-famous zoo, as it was billed. Once inside, we wandered from animal to animal, hanging on the cool bars, pressing our faces to the glass. It was impossibly hot. The monkeys swung listlessly from their pretend trees. We rested under a sign that said 'Welcome to Africa, Home of the Lions.' My mother told me about an elephant named Buddy that had escaped from a circus in Philadelphia and trampled a boy to death. 'My head hurts. I'm tired of this sun,' I said. Inside the Reptile House, kids threw pennies at the alligators' heads. Loud music blared over the speakers. After a while, we gave up on the animals and went to the refreshment stand, where we sat under umbrellas and drank lemonade. Nearby, peacocks roamed between the tables, sidestepping the screaming kids who tried to grab them.

We went home and tried to take a nap, but it was too hot. It was always too hot. Too hot for the park, too hot for a bike ride, too hot to get in the car. I dreamed of the perfect swimming hole, cool and clear, where fish darted past my feet and there were no snakes skimming across the dark water. The next day my mother surprised me with a little wading pool shaped like a turtle. We dragged it onto the balcony, then filled it cup by cup with water from the sink. When I looked down, there were smiling fish between my toes.

In New Orleans, my mother said, you could fall in love with a zombie and never know until it was too late. The man who worked at the grocery store was a zombie; so were the garbage man and the woman who sold stamps on the street. It was the nature of a zombie not to know that he was one, she explained. A person became a zombie when a voodoo priest came to his grave and dug him up with a magic spell. Then he took him away to work for free, because a zombie will work and work without complaint. In Haiti, zombies worked cutting sugarcane, but in America they worked at all the jobs no one else wanted, my mother said. They worked in the fast-food restaurants and in Laundromats. They cleaned houses and sold shoes. Sometimes they worked at tollbooths on highways and you glimpsed them for just a moment as your car passed by.

'What is the magic spell?' I asked my mother. 'How do you get away?'

'Each person is made up of five things,' she told me. 'There is your physical body, which is called the *corps cadavre*, and the *n'ame*, which holds the body together. Next comes the *gros bon ange*, the life force which animates a person, and the *ti bon ange*, which is what we would call the soul. But most important of all is the *z'etoile*, which is your star of destiny. When a person dies, the *z'etoile* flies up to the sky and stays there, storing a person's destiny for future incarnations. You might come back as a person or a dog or even a tree. It all depends on what your star of destiny says.'

I wanted very much to see a zombie. Everywhere we went, I looked for the glazed eyes and listless walk which were the telltale signs. The only thing that would bring back a zombie's memory of his former life was the taste of salt, my mother said. Because of this, we always carried packets of it in our pockets and in the glove compartment of the Purple Pig.

We saved salt to put in the time capsule we were making too. My mother had gotten the idea for it from my father's show, the one about the space shuttle that broke up into different parts. One of the parts was a silver time capsule that shot like a bullet into space. Inside it were books and photographs and a letter from the President. Also, packets of seeds in case the people on other planets were starving to death. One day we might land on Mars, my father said, and be surprised to find it covered with wheat.

I wanted to launch our capsule into space, but my mother said it would just fall back to the ground, so we were going to bury it, instead. Already, we'd dug a hole in the backyard and covered it with leaves. We'll have to write a note, my mother said, explaining everything.

We put a box on a table in the middle of the living room.

Every day, I thought of something new to put inside it. So far, I'd put in my 'I am the future!' button and a cockroach I'd shellacked with rubber cement. A dinosaur would recognize a cockroach, my mother told me, and one day aliens will too.

Mostly, she put pictures in the box. There was one of my parents getting married, and another of all of us at the beach floating around in inner tubes. My mother said that one day these pictures won't make any sense because no one will get married or swim in the ocean anymore. Everything will be inside, she told me, and we'll all live in huge buildings connected to one another by tunnels. When you want to see a wild animal, you'll go to a special museum and put quarters in a machine for a light to come on and shine on a wolf or a bear or a bird. As long as you put in money, the light will stay on, but if you stop, even for a minute, the room will go dark. By then, our skin will be thin as paper from staying inside and we won't even remember that we once told time by the sun. All the tunnels in the buildings will lead to subways which will be the same, only faster. You'll just touch a button when you want to get on or off.

One night, my mother put all the photographs from the album in a plastic bag and wrapped it all the way around with tape; then she put everything in another plastic bag and wrapped it up again. By the end, there was so much tape you couldn't see the pictures anymore. Just a little piece of my father's mouth that she had missed before. After she went to bed, I went back and scraped the tape off his eyes, so he could see in the dark.

On my mother's thirty-fifth birthday, we buried the time capsule in the backyard. The box was made out of a special kind of metal that could survive any kind of disaster known to man. It could survive a terrible fire or an earthquake or another age of ice, she said. Someday, a thousand years from now, someone would dig it up and know that we were here.

We went to the bar to give Wink some cake, but for once he wasn't there. 'Where could he be?' my mother asked. 'Do you think he's left us all alone?' We drove to the railroad tracks near his house and watched the trains roar past. He could be on that one or that one or that one, she said.

When we got back to the apartment, my mother couldn't sleep. Something was wrong with her heart, she said. At night, she could feel it racing and had to lie very still until it stopped. Also, she had a cut on her knee that wouldn't heal, and this was proof that something was wrong. She pulled off her Band-Aid and showed me her knee. It was purplish blue where she had banged it on the coffee table playing horse. 'Blue is the real color of blood,' I told her, 'but it turns red as soon as air touches it.' My mother pinched at the skin on her knee. 'You're just like your father, aren't you?' she said.

The next night, when we went to the Bitter End, there was a new bartender there. 'Where's Wink?' my mother asked. The man behind the counter shrugged. He had a handlebar mustache and small dainty hands. 'Eloped to Las Vegas with some girl, I think.' My mother excused herself and went into the back room. She snapped a pool cue and broke the clock. The clock had white horses on it that ran toward a waterfall. They stopped running when the glass cracked. My mother came back and threw twenty dollars on the bar. 'What the hell?' the new bartender said. My mother checked her lipstick in the mirror behind him. Then she drove us home in the stinking car.

151

When we got back to the apartment, she fell asleep right away for once. I knelt beside her and watched her eyes fluttering beneath her lids. Once, at church, she had knelt before the minister for a blessing and he had placed his hand on her head and said, *For all the world we are wreathed in splendor, high and low.* When my mother passed out on the couch, I touched her hands and face and blessed her like this.

But the next morning it seemed that she had forgotten everything. She told me she was in love with a man she had never met who'd written the inscription in a book she'd found. 'Where did you find the book? What was it called?' I asked her. 'It was called *Thrum*,' my mother said. 'It had a green cover with a Ferris wheel on the front. How do you think I can find this man?'

Later, when I consulted the book of dreams, it said:

LOVE

To dream of loving one person above any other denotes a secretive and greedy nature. The love of animals indicates contentment and the love of children joy. For a time, fortune will crown you.

My mother said, 'Why don't you look at me when you talk to me? You never look at me.' We were in the bar with the pickled eggs. The bartender stopped smiling when he saw her, and walked away. My mother got up and went outside. I followed her. It was raining. Tree branches blew across the street. We held newspapers over our heads and ran. When we got home, there was a note on the door that said: *Final Notice.* My mother went out on the balcony and watched the rain tear through the trees. Balloon animals bobbed across the dark pool. In the back room, the wind slammed a window shut. My mother came and stood in the doorway. With wet hands, she held the hair back from my face. In the corner, the miraculous corn shone like a light. Someone was getting in a car somewhere, I thought, and driving toward us in the dark. 'I want to see you,' my mother said. 'Look at me.'

24

It wasn't quite light out when we left. Under the slow falling moon everything looked blue. The blue hour, my father used to call it, but he had meant another time, the time just after the sun went out. I closed the door behind us. 'So this is it,' my mother said. 'The day has dawned.' Before I woke up, she had packed everything in the car. She carried the last bag to the door and let herself out. The cool air smelled of the river. The sidewalk was wet. It must have rained in the night, I thought, while we slept. But I hadn't slept at all, only watched the hands of the clock tick their way around.

I got in the car. The night before, my mother had tied the corn on top of the car again. 'For luck,' she said. I had thought someone might take it while we slept, but it was still there, shining in the dark. The white dog my mother called Ghost was picking through garbage in the abandoned lot. My mother called to him as she passed, but the dog didn't look up. He had a bag of bread in his mouth and was shaking it from side to side like a rat. Ghost, she called again. Ghost. A paper boy appeared and got on a bike made for a girl. I watched him as we waited for the light; he had a thin wisp of a mustache and handlebars that curved like swans. He saw us and smiled shyly. The basket of his bike was covered with flowers, red and green. The light changed.

The boy sped past us, pedaling furiously. My mother roared ahead. In the rear-view mirror, I could see the boy waving to us. It was like a dream, the way he got smaller and smaller, then disappeared.

That night, my mother drove through a tunnel and I was terrified that I would lose the voice of the man on the radio who had been speaking to me quietly and secretively through two states. The voice was like my father's, coming from every direction at once, the vents, the windows, the crack in the door. *He had always believed himself to be an honorable man*, the voice said, *but on the day of the piano player's trial, his honor let itself out like a cat*. When we entered the tunnel, the man's voice dimmed, but did not go out. Instead, it seemed he was speaking through snow.

We drove and drove. The Purple Pig smelled like a dead thing. The mildew grew secretly at night while we slept, I knew. Hold your nose, my mother said each morning when we got in.

My mother never tired of driving. She liked to listen to the radio and watch the towns go by. Sometimes cars honked at us as they passed. Whenever this happened, my mother sped up to see who was inside, but it was never anyone she knew.

In a motel gift shop, my mother bought a map of America and spread it out for me to see. Where were we going, I asked her. To Disneyland, she said. She told me that we would visit the last dusky seaside sparrow and stay in the castle where Snow White lived. But wasn't that bird at Disney World, not Disneyland, I asked. It flies back and forth between the two, my mother explained. She took my hand and smiled at me. Soon we'll be there. Very, very soon, she said. She mapped out our route with a yellow marker. Anaheim, she circled at the end.

But that night before bed, my mother pushed the Disneyland brochures away. Come with me to Thailand, she said. We'll ride elephants through the shining streets. We'll earn our keep plumping pillows in an opium den. We'll dance on stage in costumes made of hundred-dollar bills. We'll call ourselves the Beautiful Twins.

In the morning, we stopped at a restaurant and one of our credit cards was refused for the first time. My mother said that this was a sign we should eat less and drive more. In supermarkets, we listened for the voices of the dead animals calling to us. We drank only rainwater that she collected in a can by the side of the road. The hungrier we got, the more superstitious. We ate only bread that came in the package with the star. 'We're evolving,' my mother said. 'Soon we'll need nothing but air to live.'

We were halfway to California when my mother explained about her luck. 'It used to come so easily,' she said. 'Then I lost my lucky shoes.' She'd found the shoes in a junk shop in New Orleans. Her initials were carved into the sole of one of them. 'AW,' it said, just like that. She bought the shoes and that night she fell in love. His name was Michael and she knew he was the one the minute he walked in the room.

'How could you tell?' I asked. I looked out the window. Outside, the desert was completely dark. We could be on the moon, I thought.

'I just knew,' my mother said. 'Before I even talked to him, I knew.'

That night in the desert, we stayed in a motel called the Cactus Chateau where my mother said she and Michael had stayed. In the morning, when we came out to the car, my mother said that everything had changed. Someone had taken our sleeping bags and replaced them with identical ones which were older and more soiled, she told me. Also, one of her favorite dresses had a tiny tear in it that had never been there before. She showed me her lacquered jewelry box and the small chip on the side that had happened while we slept. Only the corn on top of the car still looked new. It's because it's one of a kind, she said. They must have had trouble with that.

I stood next to the car and looked at all the things my mother said had been changed, but I couldn't remember how they'd been before. I threw my bag into the car. Inside was a toothbrush, my detective kit, and the book of dreams.

All the next day, my mother talked about Michael. She had an idea that we should go to Joshua Tree and look for clues where he'd disappeared. She said if his car was still there it might have melted into the sand by now. Something that was hidden before could be glinting in the sun. You're my private eye, Grace, she told me, but I didn't want to go. I got out the map and showed her how far it was from Disneyland. Don't worry, I know a shortcut, my mother said.

We were a hundred miles outside of Joshua Tree when she suddenly stopped talking about him. It was as if the marker we'd passed had been a sign. Before, she had said Michael always liked the desert at night, or Michael found a coyote skull over there, or Michael kept two lizards, but after the sign she was silent. In the distance, I could see lights. There were no other cars on the road. My mother drove so fast the car began to shake.

'Charles Manson's ranch was around here somewhere,' she said. 'Remember him, he was the one who killed the pregnant movie star.' She waved her hand in the air.

'He thought he was the devil.'

My mother frowned. 'No, that's not true. Who told you that?' She fiddled with the radio, but there was only static.

'No one,' I said. 'I read it in a book.' I had seen a photograph of one of the Manson girls, grown up and a housewife now. The girl had a faint scar on her forehead where she had once carved a cross like Charlie's. When the interviewer asked what she told her children about the scar, she said, I tell them Mommy fell on a cookie cutter.

My mother sighed. 'What was smart about Manson was the way he broke up all the families. The kids belonged to everybody and the mothers were only allowed to talk to them in gibberish so they wouldn't get attached.'

'What did they say?' I asked.

'Nonsense words, I guess. Elterhay, elterskay, who knows?' She found a station on the radio that played scratchy Mexican music.

She told me how when she was little her father had taught her the opposite names for everything as an experiment. 'Dog,' she said when she saw a cat. 'Too light out,' she said when he took her camping under a starless sky. On her first day of school, her teacher told her to take a chair and she sat on the table, instead. She ended up being held back a year and her father had to reteach her everything.

'Why is a table the opposite of a chair?' I asked. We passed a sign for the park. 'They're approximate opposites,' my mother said.

We passed a restaurant shaped like a castle. I begged to stop, until finally my mother gave in and turned around. Inside, people were wearing paper crowns and eating steak with their hands. There was a sword stuck in a stone outside this restaurant and beneath it a thousand-dollar bill in a glass case. My mother stopped and tried it, but it wouldn't budge. 'This place is a rip-off,' she said. She paid for the meal with our last hundred-dollar bill.

It was late afternoon by the time we made it onto the highway. 101 degrees, the bank sign said. We drove without talking. I felt a little sick. After a while, my mother rolled down the window and stuck out her head. The car swerved across the empty road and I gripped the seat until my mother put her head back inside the car. The engine made a faint sputtering noise. My mother turned on the radio and sped up until the dunes outside passed in a blur. I thought that she was like a dog in that she loved to ride in the car.

Outside, there was nothing to see but sand. I peeled my legs off the sticky seat. The heat felt like a hand pressing against me. 'How long until Disneyland?' I asked.

My mother didn't answer. When I asked again, she waved my question away. We passed a billboard that said 'Joshua Tree, 10 miles.' 'We never should have come here,' my mother told me. 'I should have known.'

In the distance, there was a patch of water shimmering on the road. As we drove toward it, it disappeared.

'Did you see that?' my mother said. 'Over by the sign?' Down the road, it appeared again, a ghost of blue water.

My mother pulled over. She took a picture, then got back in the car. 'Michael would have loved this,' she said. 'He always wanted to see one.' I knew that we had passed into Michael's desert again, where every rock and cactus was named for him. My mother seemed happy for the first time since we'd left the Cactus Chateau. I imagined a woman walking down a street somewhere, wearing her lucky shoes.

25

We were two hours from Disneyland when my mother saw a poster at a gas station that made her change her mind. She ripped it off the bulletin board and showed it to me. 'Look, Grace,' she said excitedly. 'It's the festival Edgar told us about. It's happening just a little ways from here.' She took out a piece of paper she kept folded up in her wallet. 'The Burning Man!' the flyer said. My mother got out a map and retraced our route. We had missed it by just a little bit, she said. I looked at the place she'd circled and at the star I'd made on the map for Anaheim. I cried and banged on the door to be let out, but she ignored me. Even when I stopped crying, I refused to talk to her. 'Fine,' my mother said. 'I've had just about enough of you.'

We rode for hours in silence, but when we reached the spot in the desert filled with lights and cars and strange machines, I forgot for a moment that I hadn't wanted to come. It looked like a carnival without any rides. We drove past a huge stick man made of scaffolding. It rose forty feet into the air, tethered to the ground by thin wire cables. At its feet, hundreds of people were gathered around. 'It's the Burning Man,' my mother said. 'Tonight they'll light it on fire.' We parked behind a line of cars and began to walk. My mother insisted on bringing the corn, so we walked slowly, dragging it along. Everywhere, there was the sound of drumming. A woman ran by covered in white body paint, a tattoo of a vine on her back. My mother pointed to a man whose lips and ears were pierced with heavy silver rings. He was carrying a small boy in his arms and handing out flyers. My mother took one and put it in her purse. 'Nice corn,' the man said. I noticed we were the only ones wearing shoes. We made our way through the crowd toward the Burning Man. At its base were flowers and bones and offerings of food. We dragged the corn through the crowd of people and left it at the Burning Man's feet. As we approached, it lit up in blue and spread its arms like wings. I counted its neon ribs, ten in all. 'It's pretty,' my mother said. I expected it to walk toward us, but it stood still, a pale blue skeleton in the light.

In the afternoon, my mother took me to watch two machines fight. One machine had a live rabbit running in a wheel, and the other one shot flames and blue sparks into the air. My mother and I stood a little apart from the crowd. Everyone was quiet while the machines fought. They made a loud sound whenever they touched. I was a little afraid of the one with the sparks. It was taller than a house, but not as big. The rabbit was scared too. It seemed to run faster and faster in its wheel. I watched the machines clank and spark. After a long time, they stopped. Little pieces of paper fell from the sky. My mother picked up a scrap and read it. I could see people above on the scaffolding and then the white paper floating down. Some people caught the paper in their hands. It was almost the end of dusk. A man with a silver hand went over to the machines and covered them with a tarp. After a moment, he lifted the tarp and took the rabbit out of its cage. He petted the rabbit and held it to his face. My mother said that the man had lost his hand in an explosion. She said that he stole all the parts he needed for his machines because he didn't believe in work. Something in my mother's voice made me afraid she would leave and go with him. Her hand was cold. I thought it had turned to metal in the dark.

That night, we walked a long ways into the desert because my mother wanted to find a place to sleep where no people were. 'I think I saw Michael tonight,' she told me. 'He left a flower for the Burning Man.' The moon appeared suddenly over the dunes. My mother took my hand. 'Here,' she said, pointing to a place at the bottom of one of the dunes. We spread out our sleeping bags and lay down on the sand.

In the middle of the night, my mother got up and put on her unlucky shoes. 'Go back to sleep,' she whispered. She took her keys, but left the water and chocolate behind. Even with the full moon, it was dark where we'd camped. I could see my mother's footprints, leading up to the top of the dune, then disappearing.

She was gone a long time. I was suddenly afraid that she had left me there. I remembered the story she had told me about the spirit houses and the children who waited alone inside them.

There were flyers scattered across the sand where my mother had emptied out her pockets. Earlier we had gone from booth to booth, collecting them. The moonlight made everything look as if it had a line drawn around it. I thought of astronauts walking on the moon. How far away the Earth must have seemed. Blue for the oceans, green where people were.

I picked up the flyers. *The Time Has Come for Voluntary*

Human Extinction! the first one said. I opened it and inside was a test you could take to see how much you loved the Earth.

ECO DEPTH GAUGE

HOW DEEP IS YOUR COMMITMENT TO OUR PLANET?

1. *Superficial: We should take good care of our planet as we would any valuable tool.*
2. *Shallow: We have a responsibility to protect the Earth for future generations.*
3. *Knee-deep: The planet would be better off if there were fewer people on it.*
4. *Deep: Wilderness has a right to exist for its own sake.*
5. *Deeper: Wildlife has more right to exist than humans do.*
6. *Profoundly deep: We are too great a threat to other forms of life. Our species should be phased out.*
7. *Radically deep: Human extinction now, in order to give Earth a chance. A painless extermination is needed.*
8. *Abysmally deep: Humans are a plague to the Earth and deserve to die an immediate and painful death. A horrible disease from outer space would be the most fitting end.*

Someone had circled number 7 in red pen. I folded up the flyer into a tiny square and buried it in the sand. I thought of how my mother had said that scientists should create a superpredator to hunt humans and give the rest of the animals a chance. I shone my flashlight over the sand and into the dark night, but there was no sign of her. In the distance, I heard a strange crackling sound like something running through underbrush. I took out the book of dreams to calm myself. Dreams beginning with L, my finger landed on.

164

LOVELY

If through the vista of dreams, you see your own fair loveliness, Fate bids you with a gleaming light, awake to happiness.

I stood up and followed my mother's footsteps over the sand dune until they stopped. Then I walked toward the sound of cars in the distance. The moon slid behind a cloud. There's never any weather on the moon, my father had told me once. I walked and walked, but the hum of the cars kept moving just out of reach. Everywhere I looked were the crooked shapes of desert trees. I tried to pay attention to the order of things. Remember the three trees bent like dancers. Remember to walk back toward them. Walk away from the bent cross, back toward the bowing man. But sometimes when I turned suddenly, it seemed the trees had rearranged themselves. I stood still and let the night tilt around me.

When I opened my eyes again, the sound of the cars had turned into the sound of the wind. I walked and walked. After a while, I cleared a place at the bottom of a dune and lay down. Sand stung my eyes. I wondered how long I had been gone and if my mother would ever find me. I took off my shoes and laid them out neatly beside me. Above me, the stars moved slowly away. If you lie down in the sand, you might fall asleep and die, I remembered, but of course that was wrong, that was a story about snow. Once my mother had asked me, 'Is it better to burn to death or freeze to death?' and the right answer was freeze because at the very end there was a trick that made you think you were warm.

26

I woke up at dawn to the sound of my mother's voice. In the distance, I could see her making her way toward me. I stood up, unsteady on my feet. It's a mirage, I thought, but she kept walking toward me. 'Where have you been?' she said, as if I was the one who had gone away. Her cheeks were wet. 'All night I looked for you.'

I told her I didn't want to stay in the desert anymore. I could hear the machines fighting again and the sound of people cheering. My mother rolled up our sleeping bags. She didn't say anything about where she'd gone, but on her wrist was a copper bracelet I'd never seen before. When everything else was packed, she took it off and buried it in the sand with all the flyers from the booths. We walked back to the car. During the night, someone had covered the hood with pennies. My mother carefully collected them and put them in her purse. As we drove off, I could see people dancing around the base of the Burning Man. Why are they doing that, I asked her. They think they're living in the last days, she said.

The next night, we stayed at a hotel that pretended to be a lighthouse. That's what it was built to look like, at least. There were shells on the dresser and a sprinkling of sand on the shower floor. Above the bed was a picture of the beach at sunset, with footprints along the water's edge. First there were two sets of footprints and then there was only one. The picture bothered me. I remembered it as part of a story my grandmother had told me once, a story I hadn't liked. There was a small television in the room, and two narrow beds. My mother poured herself a drink from the bottle she had brought with her. Somewhere along the way, I had started to think there might be a message in the bottle, but when my mother reached the bottom there was only glass. Still, there had been a moment when I had been sure I'd seen the tiny face of the woman who'd gone to sea inside.

My mother fumbled around in the desk for a pad and pen. She would leave a message in the bottle, she said, and I could send it out to sea. She stuffed the paper in the bottle and we went outside. Behind the hotel was a wreck of a beach. We walked across it to where the ocean began. I felt like a spy waiting for a secret messenger, but the sand was empty. My mother threw the bottle into the sea. 'There,' she said, swaying slightly in the wind. 'There.' In the moonlight, I could see our footprints in the sand, curving away from the hotel.

That night, as I fell asleep, I remembered the story that went with the footprint picture.

Once there was a man whose life was filled with pain and sorrow. It hadn't always been that way, but it had been for long enough that it was all the man could remember. One day he cried out, O Lord, why have you gone away from me? Why have you left my side? Jesus appeared then and showed the man a movie of his life. Beneath the scenes of other, happier days was

167

*a picture of two sets of footprints on the beach. See, Jesus said, I
walked beside you always. You were never alone. Then the
movie speeded up. There was a scene of a woman crying, an
empty crib, a dark, boarded-up house. Beneath the scenes was
the picture of the beach, but this time there was only one set of
footprints. The man cried out, How could you have left me in
my time of need? Your footsteps vanish in my darkest hour.
Why did you forsake me? My friend, Jesus said. Don't you see?
That is where I carried you.*

I woke up very early and thought of the bottle floating
out to sea. It was almost morning. Outside our window,
someone was humming. There was the sound of cars and
then all at once of rain.

My mother was still fast asleep. On the dresser was the
map she had bought in the gift shop. During the night,
she'd marked a new route on it and circled San Francisco in
red. She stirred suddenly, but she didn't wake. This was the
first time I had seen her sleep in six days. I'm becoming a
new thing, she'd told me. While she slept, I shone a
flashlight on her, half afraid of what I'd find.

I was hungry and searched the hotel room for something
to eat. I looked in my mother's pocketbook and under the
bed. In the trash can, I found half an apple and a few potato
chips in a paper bag. I took these out and ate them. At the
bottom of the bin was my Disneyland flyer covered with
grease. Also, a brochure for a hotel in Anaheim. I cleaned
these up and put them in my pocket. Across the room, my
mother tossed and turned in her sleep. She mumbled
something, then was quiet again.

I got dressed and went outside to the pay phone. In my
pocket, I had a matchbook with the hotel's name on it. I

dialed my father's number. When he came to the phone, I started to cry. 'Grace? Is that you, sweetheart?' he said. 'Grace? Just tell me where you are.'

When I got back to the room, my mother was up. 'Where did you go?' she asked. She had makeup on and her favorite dress, but her breath was rotten. 'The beach,' I said. I got back under the covers and closed my eyes.

'No, no, don't be a sleepyhead,' she said. 'We have to be on our way.'

I hid my face from her. I can be there by midnight, my father had said. Whatever you do, don't let her leave.

'I'm sick,' I whispered. I chewed on a corner of the sour blanket to make this true.

'You'll be fine,' she said. 'You just need some fresh air.' She threw the covers off me and pulled me out of bed. 'Just freshen up and we'll be off.' She paced up and down the room as if she couldn't keep still. 'No time for dawdling, Grace.'

I went into the bathroom and closed the door. I could hear my mother singing to herself in the next room. 'Five minutes,' she called. I was so hungry I felt light-headed. I leaned over the toilet and tried to throw up, but nothing came out. I wondered what to do. Was my father already on a plane? Should I leave him a clue? But how would I know where she planned to go?

I opened my mother's travel case and looked inside. I took out her pink bubble bath and poured it down my throat. It tasted like soap and perfume and made me gag, but I kept it down. I opened the bathroom door. 'All set?' my mother said. She took our suitcases out to the car. I sat on the bed and put on my shoes. Suddenly I felt the bubble bath rising up in me. I ran to the toilet and vomited up a pink mess. 'Grace, are you all right?' my mother called. She followed me into the bathroom and I threw up all over again. 'Oh my goodness, you poor child,' she said. She helped me back to my bed and tucked me in. I could still feel the sickness rolling around inside me. My mother brought a cool washcloth and held it to my face. 'Go back to sleep, my love,' she said.

I slept for a long time and woke to the sound of a key in the door. 'It's just me,' my mother said when she saw my startled look. 'I brought you soup and ginger ale.' I tried to eat the soup, but it made my stomach hurt. I pushed it away and closed my eyes again. It was hot in the room. I tried to remember what it felt like to walk outside in the snow.

My mother held her hand to my cheek. 'I think I should take you to a doctor,' she said. I told her I didn't want to go, but she wouldn't listen. She searched the room for her car keys. I looked at the clock. It was only nine. 'Please, just let me sleep a little while,' I begged.

My mother hesitated. I closed my eyes and made my breathing slow. I was afraid she might swoop down and carry me off, but after a while I heard her turn on the TV. I counted to a thousand, then I opened my eyes. My mother was watching a movie about Louis XIV, the Sun King. Afterwards, she seemed excited and talked on and on about all sorts of things, but she didn't say anything more about the doctor.

'Do you realize that back then everyone was completely

filthy? Even the king's wigs were filled with bugs and dirt,' she said. 'Meat was so rotten that spices were as valued as gold. Often, when a man undid a woman's corset, he was so overpowered by the smell of her that he fainted and had to be revived with smelling salts.'

She stood up and paced around the room. Then she grabbed a pencil off the table and waved it like a sword. 'Have you ever seen a duel, Grace?' she asked. 'Imagine, if you can, two horribly smelly men meeting in a square to fight. They insult each other cleverly while all around them spectators cheer. Then they walk ten paces and turn. The last one to draw his pistol is shot dead. Then everyone goes inside and has a feast.'

'Why do they duel?' I asked.

'Because of a woman, of course,' she said. 'At the feast, the woman who caused all the trouble is given a place of honor at the table and between courses she clasps the victor's knee.' A car pulled into the parking lot and my mother paused. We could hear it idling outside the window, then it turned off.

'Of course, the dead man lay dreaming,' my mother said. 'For that is precisely what love is.' She sighed and held the pencil to her lips. She looked at me oddly as if I was a stranger to her. 'One day you'll be just like me,' she said. 'Do you know that?'

She told me that at the end of death there was a long tunnel and in it awaited everyone you ever loved. But if you never loved anyone there was just an empty room. You went into the room, which had many beautiful things, and you waited there for someone. Time passed easily in this room, she said, and so it was always a surprise to learn that so much had passed.

Someone knocked on the door. My mother drew her pencil like a sword. 'Who goes there?' she called.

'Anna? Is that you?' my father asked.

My mother looked at me and then she looked away. 'Come in, Jonathan,' she said and unlocked the door.

27

My father paid a man five hundred dollars to drive the Purple Pig home. He took it to the car wash to get the smell out, but it didn't work. 'Jesus Christ,' the man said when he picked it up. 'What died in here?'

On the way to the airport, my mother didn't talk to anyone. My father took her hand in his. His hair was gray at the roots where the dye had worn off. 'You're nothing but bone, Anna,' he said. She didn't tell him she was evolving. She just looked out the window at the empty sand. 'How did you find us?' she asked him finally. 'Credit-card receipts,' he said.

On the plane, I ate steak and mashed potatoes and seven bags of peanuts. My mother turned and looked at me. 'I see you've recovered,' she said.

I watched clouds drift past my window. After a while, it was too dark to see anything. I tried to sleep, but I was afraid something would happen if I closed my eyes. Across the aisle, my father was speaking to my mother in a quiet voice. He talked and talked to her, but she didn't say a word.

In the middle of the night, my father pointed to his

watch and said, 'Look, Grace, we lost an hour. Where do you think it went?'

I looked at my father's watch and then at my own. 'Did we lose it in the desert?' I asked, thinking of the darkness there. My father laughed and shook his head.

'He came while you were sleeping,' my mother said, 'and stole your hour away.'

Later, on the way back from the airport, she handed me a note. *YVNE*, it said. I knew it was Annic, but I couldn't translate it from memory. I stared at it for a long time, hoping to remember, but nothing came to me. Finally, I put the note in my pocket and went to sleep. As soon as we got home, I went upstairs and got out my decoder key. LIAR, it meant.

For three days after we got back, my mother wouldn't come out of her room. My father left food and flowers outside the door and slept on the couch in the living room. Sometimes she'd sneak out in the middle of the night to take the flowers, but she always left the food. I had an idea that my mother might talk to Edgar, but whenever I called his house there was no one home. My father said he hadn't heard a word from him since we left for New Orleans.

On the fourth day, my mother came out of her room. She said that she had seen a man in the street beneath the yellow light who beckoned to her repeatedly. His face was orange, she told me, and his body was striped like a bee's. But as soon as she went to the door, he vanished.

That night, my father made a list entitled *What You Believe/What Is in Fact True* and wrote on the right side: *The*

174

man you saw was most likely a crossing guard, guiding neighbor-hood children across the street.

My father drove to the library and checked out a stack of psychology books. Then he made my mother take a test he found in one of them. He showed her pictures of a man and a woman and told her to arrange them into a story. The pictures were in black-and-white. There was a woman standing alone, then a man came in the room carrying flowers, then there was a picture of the flowers on the floor and the man and woman standing apart.

My mother told the story like this: flowers on the floor, woman standing alone, man entering with flowers, man and woman standing apart. 'What led up to this?' my father asked, pointing to the flowers on the floor. 'The expression on her face,' my mother said.

The next day, he took her to a doctor, who said her brain wasn't working properly because it was missing a kind of salt. He said this after my mother stayed up all night and made me a gingerbread house out of frosting and dimes. On the way home, my mother threw the pills he had given her out the window and threatened to jump out of the car, but my father hit the electric locks before she could. Later my mother wrote furiously on the *What You Believe/What Is in Fact True* list until she fell asleep. When I was sure she was out, I poured a little bit of salt in her ear. Now she'll remember her old life, I thought.

That night, my father told me if my mother didn't improve he would have to take her to the hospital. 'We'll have to be strong, Grace,' he said.

But the next morning my mother came out of her room and announced she would make pancakes. I thought she looked very pretty, expertly flipping them through the air.

175

Her eyes were ringed with purple because she hardly ever slept anymore. My father stood tentatively in the doorway. 'Anna,' he said, 'there's a meteor shower tonight. Would you like to watch it with us?'

'I can't,' she said. 'I have a date with the crossing guard again.' She laughed and kissed him on the cheek. He laughed too. Later, when the lights streaked across the sky, my father sang, 'Chicken Little's mistake was an easy one to make,' and danced with my mother on the wet lawn. 'La di da, my love,' she said, the night before she disappeared.

28

T he following winter, I moved with my father to Connecticut so we could be closer to the show. The house he rented was all white. Every single thing inside it was brand-new. The downstairs was so big there was one room we didn't even go into. In this room, which my father called the parlor, there were plastic covers over all the chairs.

One night I filled in for the question girl, who was having her tonsils out. I stood in the middle of a fake blizzard and asked why the seasons changed. After the show ended, we went outside and suddenly it was night. 'It's the winter solstice,' my father said. 'There is less light today than any other day.' When we got back to my father's house, he sent me to bed early because of the dark.

Later I woke up and heard my father talking to someone in the kitchen. My mother had just been gone a little while, but already it seemed he talked only to me. When I went downstairs, there was a woman sitting at the kitchen table, eating a cracker. She had dark red hair and a long, pinched face. I had seen her the day before, working lights for the show. Foxface, I called her secretly.

My father got up to fix her a drink. I stood back a little from the door so he wouldn't see me. Foxface reached into her purse and took out a cigarette. 'Watch this, Jonathan,' she said. She struck a match against her teeth and it caught fire. She lit a cigarette. 'Amazing,' my father said. He took a step toward her, then saw me in the doorway. 'Go back to bed, Grace,' he told me. I turned and looked at her. She stubbed out her cigarette and held out a hand. 'Look who it is,' she said. 'Ask me a question, sweetheart.'

The next morning, when I woke up, she was gone. It had snowed for the first time overnight. I drew a picture of a pine wreath and hung it on the door. The real one was back home at the house in Vermont. When my father saw the picture, he asked me what I wanted for Christmas. I said that I wanted to buy a star and name it after my mother. I had read that for fifty dollars you could do this.

My father shook his head. 'That's not what stars are for,' he told me. 'I don't think she would have wanted such a thing.' I hated the way he never said her name anymore. 'Your mother,' he said sometimes, but that was all.

I went to my room and got the ad out. It showed a boy standing at a window, holding a small star to his chest. 'We don't have time for this now, Grace,' my father said. 'We're already late.' He took the ad away from me and put it in a drawer.

I put on my shoes very slowly and followed him to the car. There was nothing on the radio but Christmas music. The car skidded a little on the icy street. My father turned the radio off. We drove over a bridge and past a church where a man was herding sheep onto a stage. A kid wearing silver wings ran across the snow. 'Look,' my father said. He slowed down and the boy darted past.

We drove by the frozen river and the houses decorated with white lights. No one had lawn ornaments here. I thought of my mother and her garden gnomes. My father hummed a little under his breath and tried to catch my eye.

'Why don't we get a dog, Grace?' he said. 'You could name it anything you wanted. You could name it Laika like the first dog in space.'

'That dog died,' I said.

'Anything,' my father said. 'You could name it anything.'

I looked out the window. Already it was getting dark. Once my mother had told me that she had been named Anna because it sounds the same backwards and forwards. My grandfather liked words like that and had wanted me to be named Eve or at least Lily so I could be called Lil. He died just before I was born and my mother said that this was one of the last things he asked her.

The last thing my mother asked me was this: 'Do you know how to run the dishwasher, Grace?' I didn't and she showed me how. That night, my mother went to bed very early. The next morning, I heard my father outside calling for her. I went to the window. My father stood on the grass in his pajamas. 'Anna,' he yelled. 'Anna.' A car glided through the light, silver like a fish. When my father saw me at the window, he picked up the paper and came inside. It was just getting light out. 'Your mother's disappeared,' he said. He looked bewildered, as if she had vanished in a puff of smoke instead of in his green car. There was no note, but there was a shell on the kitchen table that hadn't been there before. It was white with a thin crack down the middle that forked like a lizard's tongue. My father touched it lightly. 'Don't worry. She'll be back soon,' he said.

When she wasn't, I took the shell upstairs and hid it in the pocket of my old coat, so I could find it later and be surprised.

Two days passed and still there was no sign of her. My father went to the police and filed a missing-persons report. He slept in the living room, next to the phone, but it never rang. Sometimes he would pick it up and listen just in case.

Later they found my father's green car in the lake by the fire station. They pulled it from the water with a crane, but my mother wasn't in it. Men in small boats dragged the water with nets all through the night. For weeks, they looked for her, shining lights across the lake. Finally, they gave up and called off the search. I wasn't surprised that they hadn't found my mother in the lake. They couldn't find a forty-foot monster either, I knew.

Soon after that, a policeman came to the door. He had an old brown coat in his hands. This was the coat my mother wore when she worked in the garden. The policeman told my father that when they found the coat its pockets had been filled with stones. He laid the coat gingerly on the table. It smelled like a wet dog. I reached my hand into the pockets but the stones were gone. My father took the coat and put it away. He said that my mother got the idea for the stones from a woman who wrote a book. Then he locked himself in the bathroom and turned all the water on. I put my ear to the door. 'Anna,' I heard him cry, backwards then forwards, 'annA.'

I went to my room and took the shell out of its hiding place. One end was sharp like an arrowhead. I pricked my finger on it again and again, trying to see blue, but it was like trying to catch the refrigerator light off.

WHY CAN YOU HEAR THE OCEAN INSIDE A SEASHELL?
This is just a trick your ears play on you. What you hear is not the

sound of the ocean, but rather the sound of your own blood rushing through your ears. All the shell does is amplify the sound so that you can hear it, the way a stethoscope lets you hear the beating of your heart. Some people say you hear the sea inside a shell because the shell remembers its home even when it has been taken away, but this is just a story.

It was almost dark. My father drove carefully through the icy streets. There were lighted trees in all the windows of all the houses we passed. 'What if I buy you some glow-in-the-dark stars?' he said. 'How would that be? Would you like a telescope so you can see the planets at night?'

'No,' I said.

He put his hand on mine. 'I didn't mean to be short with you before,' he said. He leaned close to me. The car smelled like birds. There was one in the back he was going to use for the show. Every time the car slowed down, it let out a squawk. I climbed over the seat and put a black cloth over its cage. 'When someone dies, their soul flies up to heaven and becomes a star,' I told the bird.

My father swung around to look at me. The bird cooed quietly in the dark. 'Did your mother tell you that?' he asked.

'Everybody knows that,' I said. 'You're the only one that doesn't.'

'Come up front again, Grace. Sit by me.'

'No,' I said.

We came to the road that led to the studio. My father turned onto it without a word. The bird grew quiet too. We pulled into the parking lot. I jumped out of the car and slammed the door. My father took the bird cage out of the back seat. 'We'll do the bird last,' he said. He tried to catch up with me, but the bird cage made him slow.

The summer I was four, my parents rented an old house on Cape Cod. Our cove was filled with jagged rocks and no one liked to go there but us. 'Who's been walking here?' my father would say when the three of us went out after dinner. Then he'd pick me up and fit my feet to the prints in the sand.

One day my father came home early from visiting friends. My mother was in the back, washing the sand from her hair. He kissed her hello, then went inside. She came and found me on the beach. 'Let's hide from your father,' she said. 'Doesn't that sound fun?' She began to walk crookedly along the sand, dragging her foot behind her. 'See, we'll leave clues,' she said. She walked backwards in her tracks toward me. 'Like this,' she said, zigzagging back toward the water. I followed her, copying her limp and adding a little hop. We lurched and peglegged down the beach, laughing to think of my father tracking such strange animals. At the end of the cove, we hid behind a rock and waited for him to find us. We waited for a long time, but he didn't come. The sun began to sink into the water. My mother held my hand so tightly it hurt. I shivered in my thin bathing suit. 'I want to go home,' I said. My mother dropped my hand. We walked back without talking. It was low tide and the gulls were flying in. There was seaweed everywhere, twisted in great clumps on the beach. I closed my eyes and walked carefully around it. 'Are you unhappy, sweetheart?' my mother said. 'What are you thinking about when you close your eyes like that?' Her voice sounded funny. Above us, a plane wrote something in the sky. I dragged my bad leg through the sand. 'I'm happy,' I said.

When my father finished with the bird, a man came and took it away. It flew out of his hands and fluttered into the rafters. Before he could catch it, the lights began to dim. My father stepped behind a curtain and the spotlight came on.

WHAT DID THE FIRST BIRD LOOK LIKE?
The entire kingdom of birds is descended from dinosaurs, feathers from their scales and wings from the second finger of their claws. The first bird, called Archaeopteryx, may have taken flight more than one hundred and fifty million years ago. It was a small crow-sized animal that wobbled over bushes and barely maneuvered among trees. But in the days when nothing else could catch flying insects, its awkward flight was good enough. It did not sing, but it may have croaked or hissed.

HOW SMALL IS THE SMALLEST BIRD IN THE WORLD?
The smallest bird in the world weighs no more than a sugar cube. It is called a bee hummingbird because its body is about the same size as a bee. Even though it is named after a bee, it would never sting you. If you tried to catch it in a jar, it would fly away. You will probably never see one, because they live only in Cuba.

I stepped out of the light. The music came up, then the applause. My father picked me up and swung me through the air. The bird flew out of the curtains and was captured in a silver net.

29

In June, we drove back to our old house in Vermont. In the back seat of the car were the books my father had brought to while away the time. How to, How to, How to, they said. We passed the lake, which was filled with picnickers. Foxface had made us bag lunches to eat on the way, but I hadn't eaten mine.

I had an idea that when we got home my mother might be waiting for us on the front porch, but when we pulled in the driveway, no one was there. The house looked smaller than I remembered. The Purple Pig was still parked on the street, covered with a tarp. My father had a new car now with a convertible top. When we rode in it, we wore sunglasses and waved to everyone like movie stars.

Inside, the house smelled musty and old. I wandered through the rooms, touching tables and chairs. I was surprised that everything was still there.

My father went out on the back steps and looked at the yard. The grass was green and the sprinklers were on. Tomato plants grew in my mother's garden. Someone had weeded the plot and made a small pile of dirt and roots beside the shed.

I walked around the edge of the garden to the old doghouse. There was a piece of wood next to it that I hadn't seen before. I knelt down and looked inside the house, but it was empty.

My father came over and picked up the piece of wood. He examined it for a moment, then threw it on the weed pile. 'Edgar's certainly done a fine job of looking after things,' he said.

We went inside and made lemonade. My father wandered around the kitchen, opening and closing drawers. 'Now, where do you suppose he's put the mail?' he asked.

We looked in all the usual places, the basket in the kitchen, the hallway table, the foot of the stairs, but there was no sign of it. Finally, I found a stack of letters on the floor beside the coatrack. Some of them had spilled over and were half hidden by scarves and boots. I gathered up the mail and brought it to my father.

He went through the pile carefully, but when he got to the end, it turned out every letter was for him. My father frowned. He looked through the mail again. 'That's odd,' he said. Usually my mother was the one who got the most mail. She liked to enter contests and was always sending away for things. *You may have already won!* was the way letters to her often began.

My father got up and fixed himself a drink. He gathered the letters from the table and put them in the basket by the door.

'Maybe she came to get her mail while we were gone,' I said.

My father looked away. 'Maybe,' he said.

The next morning, my father got out the lawn mower and worked on the grass. He weeded the garden and planted new seeds. I sat on the porch and watched him work.

'Would you like to give me a hand, Grace?' he asked.

'No thank you,' I said. I went inside and called Edgar's house again. Already I had called five times, but there was no answer. He must be on vacation, my father said.

I went across the street to spy on the blind girl. All the curtains were drawn and the car was gone. I hid in the bushes for a while, waiting for someone to come home, but no one did.

I decided to walk over to Edgar's house. I didn't expect him to be there, but when I rang the bell, he answered the door. He was dressed all in white and his hair was cut very close to his head.

'Edgar, you're home!' I said. He didn't say anything, but he let me in. He took me to the kitchen and gave me cookies and milk. I told him about the new house in Connecticut and Foxface and my week as the question girl. Also about the star I had tried to buy for my mother. Edgar nodded, but he didn't say a word.

I looked at him. His face was smooth and blank. 'Why aren't you talking?' I asked.

Edgar reached into his pocket and pulled out a card. He handed it to me. The card said:

Please be advised that I have taken a vow of silence. All necessary communications will be conducted by paper and pen.

'When did you start?' I asked him.

'January 2, 1986,' he wrote on a pad.

I calculated this in my head. I thought this must be the longest anyone had ever played the silence game. 'How come?' I asked.

Edgar shrugged.

'How come?' I asked again.

He took out a piece of paper and scribbled something on it. *'Your mother said not a word until she returns.'*

I looked at the note. 'My father says she's not going to,' I told him.

Edgar closed his eyes. I asked him what he did with all the time he saved by not talking.

He went into the living room and brought back a book. *An Introduction to the Meditative Arts*, it was called. I opened it to a picture of a man in a turban twisting himself into knots. *We pass through boredom into fascination*, the caption read.

'Can you do that?' I asked him.

Edgar nodded. He sat cross-legged on the floor. Then he flipped himself over and stood on his head. He stayed that way for a long time, much longer than I would have asked him to. I sat on the couch and watched his face turn red. His eyes were wide open, but he didn't seem to be looking at anything. I tried to be fascinated, but mostly I was bored. After a while, I tapped him on the foot. 'I want to go home,' I said.

Edgar rolled over into a somersault. He went to his mother's purse and got out her keys. He had his driver's license now, he wrote, but his parents wouldn't let him have his own car until he started speaking to them again.

In the car, Edgar gave me the book on meditative arts, even though I hadn't asked for it. When I got home, I tried to do what the man in the turban did, but whenever I stood on one foot, I fell over right away. There were hundreds of poses in the book, each one with a different name. There was Downward Dog and Warrior and Triangle and Snake. Last of all was one called Corpse, where you lay on the ground like a dead man. *Guard that you do not become attached to the things of this world*, the book said.

A few days later, a spotted dog appeared at our door. She had sad eyes and a lame paw. When I tried to pet her, she shied away, but that afternoon she came back and licked my hand. From then on, every time I opened the door, she was waiting for me. The only time she growled was when I went inside. Then she would scratch the screen and whine until I opened it again. Sometimes we played ball in the yard. She couldn't run very fast because of her hurt leg. When my father saw her limping, he came over and examined her paw. She gave it to him without complaint, as if she were having her fortune read. She had a thorn in it, my father said. I brought him the tweezers and he took it out. Later I saw her testing it out gingerly on the grass. I waited awhile, then threw the ball again; this time she ran so fast her spots were a blur. Would you like to keep her, my father asked. Yes, I said.

I named her Laika, after the first dog in space. I knew that she had come to me from far away. Sometimes, at night, I worried that she might run away again. She kicked her legs and whimpered in the dark room as if she were being chased. When she did this, I woke her up and petted her until she was quiet again. Her tail thumped out her thanks on the floor even after she had fallen asleep. I liked to sleep with her paws around me, breathing in her biscuit breath.

Laika knew three games: fetch, hide-and-seek, and rescue dog. Rescue dog was best in the snow, but we made do with just grass. I was the famous mountaineer climbing the mountain without oxygen. She was a St.

Bernard that no blizzard could scare. At the top of the compost heap, I planted my flag. Then I began the treacherous descent, buffeted by winds. Laika waited in the garden, chewing grass. She had a thermos tied to her collar that I'd fixed there before. Sometimes she got bored waiting and tried to chew it off. Halfway down the mountain, I had a terrible fall. 'Mon Dieu!' I yelled. 'Rescue dog!' I had read a book called *They Lived on Human Flesh* about what happened to people lost in the mountains. Laika ran over and licked my face. I played dead. She licked my arms and legs too. There were some apple peels and coffee grounds on my shoes and I could feel her nibbling them. I drank the lemonade she brought me, happy to be saved.

Laika brought deer bones back from the woods and hid them behind the shed. She thought I didn't know where she kept them, but when she wasn't looking, I poked around in them. So far, Laika had found eleven bones. Soon she'd have enough for a whole deer, I thought.

In the woods, Laika was as quiet as a cat. She could sneak up on squirrels until it was almost too late for them to get away. One squirrel she almost caught, but at the last minute it ran up a tree. Laika never forgot about that tree. Every time we went to the woods, she would go to it and sit patiently, waiting for that squirrel. Weeks later, she still remembered.

She had a funny idea about time, I thought. An hour or a day or a week were all the same. She didn't think the squirrel might have run away when she wasn't there. Instead, she thought he was waiting for her too. My father said that Laika believed in circular time, which meant that everything that had ever happened would happen again.

And so one day when she was walking through the woods she'd see the gray squirrel again, waiting in his patch of sun. He hadn't heard her yet, but in a moment he would and the old chase would begin. He'd race up the tree, Laika at his heels, and they'd both stare at each other until I called her away.

Was time a circle for people too, I wondered. If so, that meant my mother would drive her car into the lake a thousand times and each time would feel like new.

Laika wouldn't come for my father. Only for me. It seemed she'd forgotten about his help with her paw. When he petted her, she'd stare at him calmly, as if to say, I think we've met, but as soon as he stopped she'd walk away. Finally, he let her be. 'She's your dog now, Grace,' he said. And so she was. I fed her and walked her each morning and night. At night, she slept on the end of my bed and kept the darkness away.

Most days, we went to the lake. I told her about the monster who lived there, but she wasn't afraid. She'd swim out to retrieve the sticks I threw, then bring them back and drop them at my feet. Once I threw a stone instead and she paddled around and around in circles looking for it until I called her in. She was tired when she swam back. She lay on the beach, panting. I buried my face in her wet coat. She smelled like rain and dirt and fur. I'll never trick you again, I promised, and she licked my hand.

Sometimes I tried to get Laika to go inside the doghouse out back, but she was smart enough to see the lock and run away. What had the dog done who had lived in that house, I asked my father, but he didn't know.

Laika ran off sometimes, but she always came back. Once I went out looking for her and saw her in her secret life. She was at the junkyard, running around with the wild dogs. She found a chicken bone in the grass and ran up to the top of the hill. The other dogs followed her. She snarled and growled when they came for her bone. One got too close and she bit him on the tail. He whimpered loudly and slunk away. Laika's ears were sleek against her head and her teeth were bared. She fought the other dogs until they ran away. I called her name, but she pretended not to hear. The next day, I went back and found her sleeping in an old tire. When she saw me, she wagged her tail and ran to me as if to say, At last, I'm found!

Once Laika came, I wasn't lonely for my mother anymore. I knew that she had come back to me, wearing a different skin. Was Laika magic, I wondered, examining her pink belly and smooth paws. And she said without speaking, *No more magic than water into ice.*

For the Fourth of July, Foxface invited us to visit her at the Cape. She had rented a house on the beach that was much too big for her, she said. Don't worry, you can bring Laika, my father told me.

I didn't want to go and sulked through the long drive. When we got there, I saw that the house was an ordinary one, no bigger than ours. Foxface told my father she had rented the house from a family who left each summer because they needed the money. They had a daughter just my age, she said. It was a shame we couldn't play together. There was a picture of the girl on the mantel. She had buck teeth and brown hair in a braid. I took Laika into the kitchen and gave her some water. Then I put my things in the girl's room. She had a canopy bed and pictures of horses all over the wall. Under her pillow, I found a note that said, *Whoever you are, I hate you.* There was another taped to the radio. *Don't touch anything in my room!!!* it said. *This is not your radio!!!!!* I put the note back under the pillow and went into the hall. Laika followed me. My father's car keys were on the table. I took them and went outside with the dog. I could hear my father talking to Foxface on the beach. 'I dare you,' she was saying in a lazy voice. 'I dare you just to try.' Laika and I wandered around the backyard. It was three hours until the fireworks, but there was nothing to do.

I got in the car with Laika and turned on the radio. The top one hundred songs were being counted down. Someone had called in to dedicate a song to a deaf girl who had taught him the meaning of the word 'love.' She couldn't talk, he said, but her hands told more than words could say. The deaf girl's song was slow and pretty and it seemed a shame she'd never hear it. When the song was over, Laika whined. I saw Foxface, standing on top of a sand dune with my father behind her, laughing. They spotted me and waved. My father came over and knocked on the window. 'Where are you two going?' he asked. 'You weren't going to leave us behind, I hope.' He gave Laika a piece of driftwood to chew. 'Come for a walk with us,' he said. 'Unless you were planning to steal the car?' He held out his hand for the keys. I had an idea that someday I'd be driving down a road somewhere and someone on the radio would start talking to me.

On the way back from the Cape, my father and I stopped at a little hotel on the beach. There was a sign at the desk that said 'No Dogs Allowed. No Kidding!' but we snuck Laika in anyway. My father carried her up the stairs with his hand over her muzzle just in case she made a noise.

In the hotel room, I unpacked everything and ignored my father, who was going on and on about the pool and the Jacuzzi and the free buffet. I wasn't speaking to him anymore, but still he was speaking to me. The only thing I'd said since we left that morning was 'Watch out!' when he almost hit a car in the street.

I could hear the shower going in the next room. There was a door connecting the two rooms, but it was locked. I turned on the TV.

My father stood in the doorway and smiled at me. 'Have you banished me forever, Grace? Will you never speak a word?' He sat on the bed and took off his shoes.

Someone walked by and Laika barked. 'Shh,' I said.

'At least she likes you,' my father told the dog. He went in the bathroom to change into his swimming trunks. I looked around the room. There was a Bible in the dresser and a bowl of fruit on the table. There were eighty-seven channels on the TV. I flipped through them. People cooking. Someone building a house. A man with a parrot. A car going up in flames.

Laika sighed. She was tired and wanted me to stop walking around. Wherever I went, she had to go. I lay down on the bed and waited for her to fall asleep. It didn't take long. As soon as she did, I got up and looked out the window. There was purple sky as far as I could see. I started to close the blinds, then stopped. There were dead flies all over the windowsill. I thought of my mother and the bathtub drain. Laika stirred. If she woke up and saw the flies, she would get scared and bark, I knew. I went to the dresser and got out a piece of paper. I brushed all the flies onto it and threw them away.

Laika woke up and came over to see what I was doing.

She poked her nose into the trash can and dragged the paper out. I felt a little sick, thinking of how scared she would be. I tried to take the paper away, but she was too quick. She put it on the floor and ate the flies all at once. And that was how I learned that Laika was a dog and not my mother's star of destiny.

30

When we got back to Windler, I rode my bike over to Edgar's house. I brought the book on meditation back to give to him. His father answered the door and invited me in. He was a bald, sunburned man with tufts of hair in his ears. In one hand he held a tennis racket and in the other a drink. 'Come in, Grace. You're just in time for a surprise,' he said.

Edgar came downstairs, carrying a book on mold. When he saw me, he nodded hello. Then he went out on the porch to read.

'Not so fast, Mr. Silence,' his father said. He took Edgar's arm and led him out back. In the driveway behind the house was a beautiful silver car. It had a black top and gleaming white tires. On the hood was a ribbon and a sign that said *All Yours*.

Edgar closed his eyes, then opened them again. He walked around the car, touching everything. He stopped in front of his father and made a small bow. Then he held out his hands for the keys.

His father laughed. He put the keys back in his pocket. 'What do you say, Edgar?' he asked.

Edgar shook his head. He handed his father the silence card, but his father ripped it in two. 'I said, What do you say?'

Edgar sat down cross-legged on the grass. He looked straight ahead and breathed slow, quick breaths. Then he switched to longer ones. These were the kind people who walked on hot coals used, the book said.

His father got in the car and honked the horn. He kept honking until Edgar put his hands to his ears. Then he got out and ran his hand along the gleaming hood. 'It's a beauty, don't you think?' he said to me.

Edgar passed him a note.

'You have exactly one minute to make a decision,' his father said. 'After that, I'm taking it back.' He got in the front seat and started to count.

Edgar looked at me, then he looked at the car again. His father was counting slowly, but he was already up to ten.

Edgar closed his eyes and stood on his head, with his legs bent. I followed along in the book. Queen, that one was called. He stretched out into King, then Downward Dog, then Snake, then Fish.

'I'm up to fifty-five,' his father said.

Edgar let out a tremendous sigh. He put a finger on one side of his nostrils, breathed in and out, then switched. This he did again and again. Sometimes he made a small hum like a machine.

'For Christ's sake,' his father said. 'Sixty, going once, twice, gone.' He took out the keys and started the car.

Edgar leapt to his feet. There were grass stains all over his white pants. His father turned off the engine and stared at him. 'Well?' he said.

Edgar cleared his throat. I looked at him, but he wouldn't look at me. 'Thank you,' he said. His voice was hoarse from so much silence. There was grass in his hair and all over his clothes.

'That's more like it,' his father said. He laughed and tossed him the keys. Then he went inside.

Edgar got in and started the car; then he turned it off again. He jumped out and ran into the house. When he came back, he had a backpack and a stack of letters tied with a piece of string. He handed the letters to me. They were creased as if they'd been folded in half, but none of them had been opened.

'Your mother's mail,' Edgar said. 'I've been saving it for her.' He threw his backpack into the car and got in. He rolled up the windows and turned the radio on. Then he backed carefully out of the driveway, around his father's sailboat and his mother's watering cans.

I put the letters he'd given me in my bike basket and rode along beside him to the street. 'Where are you going?' I asked, but he wouldn't say. He put on mirrored sunglasses and rolled up his sleeves. Suddenly I remembered the impostor. 'Edgar?' I said. He paused at the end of the driveway, waiting for a car to pass. As soon as it did, he floored the gas and sped away.

I pedaled furiously on my bike, trying to catch up with him, but when I turned the corner, he was already gone.

When I got home, the blind girl was having a party. *You're 12!* the banner over her driveway said. Her father drove up and unloaded a cake and a box of soda from the back of his car. I threw my bike in the garage and called Laika to come spy with me.

Around dinnertime, everyone started arriving. Cars pulled up and parked all along our street. I wasn't invited to the party. Only kids from the blind school were. Some of them came with guide dogs. Others had canes or walked holding someone's arm. From the bushes behind their house, Laika and I watched everyone. She growled a little when she saw the other dogs, but I held her mouth shut with my hands, so she got quiet again.

From my hiding place, I could see the blind girl opening her presents. Someone had given her a hula hoop and she was feeling her way around it, trying to guess what it was. After a while, her father put it over her head and explained how it worked. She laughed and tried to hula hoop, but it kept falling to the ground. 'Like this, Becky,' her father said, holding it steady around her hips. For a moment, it caught and spun. Everyone clapped as it circled her hips.

Her mother turned on the porch light and sat under it. I could see now that not everyone at the party was blind. The ones who were were touching one another's hands and faces and standing in the dark corners of the lawn. The ones who weren't were huddled on the steps beneath the only light.

For a moment, Becky stopped in front of the bushes where we were hidden. I held Laika's mouth shut so she wouldn't whine. Becky leaned over and tied her laces. She wore a rhinestone tiara that someone had given her, and when she moved, it caught the light. Laika whimpered and shifted her weight from one side to the other.

The blind girl hesitated, then took a step back. She held her hands out in front of her as if pushing someone away. 'Hello? Is someone there?' she said.

Laika and I held our breath. Becky's mother came out of the house and rang a bell. She announced a scavenger hunt and read the list aloud. A pocket knife, a dog's dish, a fishing pole, a pair of skis. When she finished with the list, she rang the bell again. 'Remember to choose a sighted partner,' she said.

I stepped out of the bushes and took Becky's arm. 'I'll be your partner,' I told her.

'Oh,' she said, startled. 'Is that Donna?' She raised her hand to touch my face. Laika ran off to chase something at the edge of the lawn.

'I'm Donna's cousin.'

The blind girl smiled and asked my name. 'It's Anna,' I told her. 'Come with me. I know where to find a dog's dish.'

'Oh, good,' she said.

I took her arm and led her across the street. It was dark out. On the lawn of Becky's house, her mother was handing out flashlights and pairing everyone up. 'Hurry,' I told her when we reached my yard. I took her around the shed to the old doghouse. It seemed smaller than I remembered. In the kitchen window, I could see my father fixing a drink. He stared out at the dark lawn, but he couldn't see us.

I stopped in front of the doghouse and unlatched the door. 'It's inside,' I told Becky. 'You have to go in and get it. I'm too big.'

'What is it?' she asked. When I told her it was a doghouse, she laughed and got down on her hands and knees. She laid her tiara beside me on the grass, then crawled in.

As soon as she was inside, I clicked the lock.

'I think I've got the dish,' she said.

I held my breath. My heart was beating too fast. I could hear her banging around inside the doghouse.

'Why did you close the door?' she asked. 'I can't find my way out.'

I sat down on the grass and waited.

'Anna?' the blind girl said. 'Anna, are you still there?' Her voice sounded strange.

When I didn't say anything, she banged on the door and yelled, but the thick wood muffled the sound. Finally, all the noise stopped and I could hear the ragged sound of her breathing. I tapped lightly on the door.

'Yes?' she said instantly. 'Is that you, Anna?'

I didn't answer. Instead, I spoke quietly to her in the voice of a bird about the monster that had swallowed her. 'He will tear you to pieces if he hears you make a sound, but if you're quiet through the night, he will let you go.'

The blind girl banged on the wall again. 'Let me out, Anna,' she yelled. 'Please. I promise not to tell.'

I checked the lock one more time to make sure it would hold. Then I went inside and fell asleep.

It was my father who found her. He went outside to get something he'd left in the yard and heard her crying in the dark.

After he took her home, he came into my room and shook me awake. 'What's gotten into you, Grace?' he said.

I explained about the spirit houses and how by morning she would have turned into a new thing.

My father shook his head. He went downstairs and called Aunt Fe. I sat on the top step and eavesdropped on him. 'I think it might be best if she came to visit Mary and Alec for a while,' he said. When he came upstairs to tell me, I pretended to be asleep. He stood in the doorway a long time without saying anything. Then he turned off the light and went away.

31

When the crow fell, its wings jerked back once, then folded in. Alec started to cry and put down his new BB gun, which he had named Mr. Bang! and carried everywhere the day before. I cried too.

'If you didn't want to kill it, why did you shoot it?' Mary said. She hated crows because they were dirty, thieving birds. She claimed one had stolen her silver anklet, the one with the tiny jingling bells, while she slept in the hammock out back. I remembered the way she had sulked when my father offered to buy her a new one. 'He's not fooling anyone with those colored contacts,' she said.

Later Alec and I went back to the field without Mary and put the dead crow in a box filled with marbles and Alec said, 'I'm sorry, bird,' before hiding it in the hollow tree that was our secret place.

But the next day Alec had the gun again. 'It was just a dumb bird,' he said, taking aim and pretending to shoot off Mary's arms and legs one by one. Mary was asleep in the sun and smelled like a coconut. I wanted to wake her up and make her look at the bird in its box, but I knew she wouldn't want to.

I'd told Mary once about the birds' alphabet, how they darted and swooped, spelling secret words in the sky. I showed her a flock of birds flying in a V, even though it was the one letter I hated for them to make, because other people knew it too. 'That's a Y,' Mary said. 'Look, they're spelling my name. Someday I'll make my husband buy a jet and write our names in the sky.' Then she ran off to make a necklace for Laika, who was running around in circles on her chain.

Laika knew about the alphabet too. Sometimes I would take her for a walk down to the end of the dirt road and we'd sit quietly, watching the dark shiny birds dropping onto the field. After a while, I would let go of Laika's collar so she could run under the fence toward them. When she ran, the birds flew up all at once, as if they were connected by string. The way they rose up reminded me of my mother throwing her hands in the air when she was mad. *I give up*, she'd say. You win. You win. After the birds were gone, Laika would lie in the middle of the field and watch them circling above her. She never barked at them, the way she did at everything else that moved. When the last ones flew out of sight, she would roll around and around in the grass and howl. I thought that Laika must be the smartest dog in the world, smart enough to be an astronaut like her namesake, the dog who'd starved to death orbiting the moon.

One day Alec said, 'I bet my dad and your mom ran off together and she's the one who writes those stupid post-cards. He never used to talk like that.'

'But she's dead,' I said. 'She drowned in the lake.' Sometimes I dreamed of the car as a fish that had swallowed my mother.

'She could have faked that to run away. Did you ever see her close up when she was dead?'

I had to admit that I hadn't, though my father had planted a tree in the backyard in her name.

Alec plucked two feathers from the bird and gave one to me. He pricked his arm with the feather's quill until he drew blood. I did the same. We touched wrists. 'Now we're bird brothers,' he said. 'If I wanted to, I could teach you how to fly.' But he didn't want to.

Alec had found a secret cave in the woods and sometimes he let me go there with him. But he always took me on a complicated, doubling-back route so I couldn't find it on my own. The opening to the cave was so small we had to crawl in on our hands and knees, but once inside we could stand up. Alec called it the Room of Everything Good and carefully monitored what was brought into it. So far, the only things he had allowed inside were three boxes of matches, deer bones, his father's Swiss Army knife, my mother's book of dreams, assorted rocks, a comic book about a murderous plant, coins from Africa, and an old zippered jacket that we were devoted to because it was reversible. I wanted to bring the dead bird to the cave, but Alec said it would stink up everything. After a few days, he gave in and let me keep a fan made of its feathers and Scotch tape inside.

One time, near the cave but not inside it, we made a fire and burned the bad father's postcards one by one. *It took two days to drive through the desert. I wish you could have seen the way the . . .* I read before the paper went up in flames.

I decided to submit *The Encyclopedia of the Unexplained* for entrance to the cave. At first, of course, he wouldn't let me inside with it. 'Wait there,' he ordered, climbing out. He had painted his face blue with finger paint. His body was covered with mud. He crouched on the ledge and held out his hand to me. I gave him the book. He read only one page. Then he turned and climbed back into the cave with it. He sat in the corner and read with a flashlight. I climbed in and sat quietly, waiting for him to acknowledge me. He was reading the section titled 'The Book of Chance.' Finally, Alec looked at me. 'This is good,' he said, 'Listen to this.'

Mark Twain fell in love with his wife after he saw her picture painted on an ivory miniature the size of a fingernail.

Girls who turn into boys have been discovered in the Philippines. (Miss Xao Ling Ping changed from a girl to a boy during a terrible thunderstorm.)

A turtle marked by Robert Brown with his initials in 1887 was found sixty-four years later by his son-in-law.

A boy named Jean Castel fell while trying to escape German soldiers during WWI and suffered total amnesia. This happened when he was fifteen. When he was twenty-four, he fell in love with a beautiful English girl. When he asked her her name, she said it was Jean Castel. Suddenly he remembered everything.

Twelve hundred Turkish prisoners died because Napoleon Bonaparte coughed. When he coughed he said, 'Ma sacrée toux' (My confounded cough), but his officers heard 'Massacrez tous' (Kill them all). So they executed all prisoners even though they had been scheduled for release.

There was a famous pianist in Paris at the turn of the century who was born without any ears. Instead, she could hear through her mouth. She married a man whose last name was Oreille, which is the French word for ear.

After Alec closed the book, he said, 'What do you suppose the chances are that your mother and my father disappeared the same year?'

'But she didn't disappear,' I said. 'She drowned.'

'She's gone, isn't she?' Alec said. 'It just seems funny that it happened exactly that way.'

I told him that the strangest part was that my mother had picked the green car to drive into the lake. That was my father's car, the one he liked best. It had fins like a shark, I remembered, and a hood ornament shaped like a star. My mother never drove it. She always took the Purple Pig instead. When she was driving uphill, she would talk to it in pig Latin because she said that was the only language it understood. Pig Latin was one of the five languages my mother knew by heart.

It started to rain. First softly and then in sheets. I was happy to be sealed inside the Room of Everything Good behind a curtain of rain. Alec stuck his head out of the cave and let all the blue run off his face. 'I'm sick of this cave,' he said. 'Let's go outside.' We went outside and walked through the mud. There was lightning and thunder, but it was hard to tell which came first by the time we started counting. Alec walked through the woods looking for a clearing where he could be the tallest thing. That way he could be struck by lightning and see what it was like. The man in the book had been struck seven times, he said. I followed him, running a little to keep up. The rain was pouring down. When we reached an open place, I stood very still and tried to turn into a boy.

A few months after my mother disappeared, my father had taken me to a museum of ethnography. 'That means manmade things,' he explained, steering me down the narrow halls. The rooms were dimly lit; glass cases filled every corner. 'Objects Made of Stone,' one section said. Inside was a stone carved into a half-moon; the handwritten tag said: *1905, used by a South American man who claimed, with the aid of a live mouse, to cure the lame and the blind.*

'Come here, Grace,' my father said. 'I think you'll like this.' He was standing in front of a glass case labeled 'Objects Made of Birds or Parts of Birds.' There was a pair of scissors made from a bird's beak that had been twisted and sharpened, and a medicine man's staff made of brightly colored feathered heads. *Found in Africa 1957*, the tag said. My hands shook a little. I pressed them flat against the glass.

'Look,' my father said. On the wall in a special case was a small blanket made of green and blue parrots' wings. I thought that it must be meant for a baby. I wondered where birds whose wings were cut off went. They must live like moles, I thought, burrowing deep underground.

When I was very little, my mother tried to teach me to fly. I stood at the top of the stairs and spread my wings. My mother waited at the bottom with her arms outstretched. 'Fly to me,' she said, and I leapt into the air between us. But my mother always caught me. 'I was afraid you'd fly too far away,' she'd say, setting me down on the bottom step. Some days I practiced by myself. When my father saw my bloody elbows and knees, he tried to talk me out of flying. 'People aren't cut out for it,' he explained. 'Our bodies are designed all wrong.' I didn't believe him. He was the one who had told me about bumblebees, how their wings were too flimsy to support their fat bodies; yet, in the summer, they were everywhere, buzzing impossibly by.

After a few days, Mary got tired of sunbathing and dared me to steal Mr. Bang! I was happy that Mary wanted to make dares again. Since she'd turned twelve, she hardly ever did. I always took dares because I was the youngest and had to. But this was a hard one because Alec carried Mr. Bang! with him everywhere. I trailed him all day, hiding behind bushes and trees until Alec wheeled around suddenly and shot the gun into the air. 'Quit following me, why don't you?' he yelled.

Later, though, he fell asleep in the hammock with the gun beside him. I crept across the grass in the Indian way he had taught me. The gun kept catching the light and flashing like a secret code. Finally, I stood over him and quietly, quietly, reached for the gun, but when I touched it, he woke up. He grabbed my arm and twisted it hard behind my back until I started to cry. 'Crybaby,' he said. He jumped off the hammock, holding his gun in one hand and my arm in the other. He dragged me over to the tree where the dead bird was hidden and made me stand against it. 'If you want to be let back in the cave,' he said, 'you have to play this game.'

The game was called 'Will you tell?' and meant I had to stand very still against the tree while Alec shot an apple off my head. Also, I couldn't cry. Alec took a long time getting ready, finding an old crab apple, arranging it on my head, aiming and re-aiming his gun. Finally, he said he was ready. I closed my eyes. 'Wait,' Alec said. 'I have a better idea.' He ran inside and got an old dishtowel which he tied across my eyes like a blindfold. The towel smelled like fish. 'Do you have any last requests?' he said. I thought of the apple, which was no bigger than a fist. I closed my eyes so tightly I saw spots. 'Last chance,' Alec yelled. 'Ready. Aim. Fire!'

I heard the gun go off, followed by a sound like a mosquito whizzing past my head. Then everything was quiet. Behind my eyes, it was green. I wondered if I was dead. Laika started to bark. I touched the apple on top of my head. It was still in one piece. Alec took off my blindfold and threw it on the ground. 'Will you tell? Will you tell?' he said, dancing around me. I turned around. Above my head, I saw the mark the BB had made in the tree. It was no bigger than a dot.

After lunch, I told Mary about the game, though I knew that this was cheating. Mary said, 'William Tell, dummy, that's what it's called. He shot an apple off someone's head once.' Then Alec came over and gave me a necklace made of the crow's feathers to prove that I was back in his good graces. Mary said, 'I'm so sick of that dumb bird. I'm going inside.' She slammed the screen door, exactly the way we weren't supposed to. I knew she was just showing off, because nobody was home.

Alec took off his shirt and ran around and around in circles, trying to get the dog to chase him, but she was too lazy. Suddenly there was a loud roar and a plane passed overhead. I thought that my mother might be inside it, looking down at me. I raised my hand to wave, then thought better of it. 'It's only a plane,' Alec said in his

208

mind-reading way. I pretended not to hear him. I lay down in the grass next to Laika and we both played dead until the plane was gone.

On the last day of summer, my aunt drove me back to our house in Vermont. My father came out to meet us in the driveway when he heard the car pull in. He had grown his beard back and was wearing a blue shirt I'd never seen before. Laika ran up to him as if we'd been away for months, then she raced around the yard until we called her in. We went inside and had cake and ice cream. Aunt Fe wouldn't have any cake because she was on a diet where you could only eat grapefruit. 'Don't be ridiculous,' my father said.

After we finished eating, Laika wandered around the house, sniffing everything. I followed her from room to room. It was late but I wasn't tired. I went into the kitchen and listened to my father and Aunt Fe talk about people they knew. After a while, Laika settled down and fell asleep.

I went out to the garage to get *The Encyclopedia of the Unexplained*, which was still in the car. Alec had tried to keep it, but on the last day I had stolen it back from the cave.

It was too dark in the garage. There were badminton racquets in the corner that made strange shadows on the wall and a collection of old skis and snowshoes jumbled next to them. My old bike was there too. Something white in the basket caught my eye. When I went for a closer look, I saw the letters Edgar had given me the day he drove away. I got my book out of the car and put some of the letters in it. The rest I carried under my shirt so my father wouldn't see.

I went upstairs and laid them out on my bed. There were twenty-four letters, all addressed to my mother, but at the very bottom was a thin envelope with my name on it. *Ms. Grace Davitt*, it said on the front. *Urgent! Open at Once!* I had never received a letter addressed to me before. I examined it carefully, then put it aside to open last.

I divided my mother's mail into piles and opened it piece by piece. There were six credit-card offers and an invitation to the firemen's ball. There were letters asking my mother to subscribe to a magazine about birds and an entry form for a contest to win a trip to a volcano. There was a sample size of a new kind of mouthwash that came with a pamphlet about how to avoid bad breath. Also two letters from a senator asking my mother to vote for him. At the bottom of the pile was a postcard from my grandmother describing her visit to Canada. She had wanted very much to see a moose but there were no mooses to be seen, she said.

I put my mother's mail under my bed and took out the letter addressed to me. This is what it said:

Dear Grace,

Have you ever lost an hour? Daylight saving is fast approaching and 38% of Americans say the time change catches them by surprise year after year. Let us be your personal alarm clock. At 976-TIME, we have a special offer for the months of April and May. Call now.

Sincerely,
Timefinders

I put the letter under the mattress. I wondered if it might be a message from my mother in code. I remembered the night in the desert when we had lost an hour and my

mother said that my father had stolen it away. I took out the
letter and read it again. Then I went and called the number
listed at the bottom. A recording came on and said that the
number had been disconnected. There was no new number, the recording said. I had an idea that my mother might
be playing a game with me. I remembered the way she used
to race me those dark nights at the lake. Catch me if you
can, she'd call out just before she streaked ahead.

32

The lost hour. My mother drives with me to the lake. The radio is on. We are playing a game called Radio Fortune. My mother flips through the dial and stops on the third song. This is the one with the message; the first words I hear are the ones meant for me. I can hardly breathe, waiting. I make my hands into the shape of a steeple, then open the door to see all the people. A man sings, *It had to be you. It had to be you.* My mother stops the car and gets out, leaving the keys inside. The man keeps singing. I step out of the car carefully. I am wearing my best dress because we have just come from church. My mother finds a pretty stone in the snow and puts it in her pocket. Then she finds another one, speckled like an egg. Together, we make a pile of stones on the shore. My mother does a little twirl and pulls me onto the ice. The sun is shining. It's a lovely day. My mother says so and I echo back the words. Lovely. You're my silly girl, she says, smiling. My mother takes my hand. In our smooth shoes, we slip and slide across the lake.

It has rained overnight and our car looks brand-new in the sunshine. There are birds on the hood that scatter as we approach. Birds, my mother says. She holds a hand to her heart and presses where it hurts.

We drive all the way to the river. There has been a flood.

The water is still rising. Our feet are underwater, but the car glides along without a hitch. My mother puts a hand to her face. She has a headache from the night before. There is a dog swimming in the river. Also a child's pool swept in by the rains. From the bridge, we watch the water rise. People jump into the river with ropes tied around their waists. They slip under, then bob back. The dog is being swept away by the current. The pool has gotten tangled in a net. A girl tied to a rope swims to the dog and pulls him into the pool. I cover my eyes. When I turn back, the river is empty. Girl, dog, and pool are all on shore.

My mother leaves the bridge and drives toward the river. Lightning splits the sky. Water, water everywhere, she says, and not a drop to drink. We speed along the dark pier. The car makes a clicking sound as it moves across the wooden slats. Then there is nothing beneath us and we fall. The windows fill with water, mud, leaves. The car floats.

A NOTE ON THE AUTHOR

Jenny Offill was born in Massachusetts and
brought up in California and North Caro-
lina. Her short stories have appeared in
numerous publications including *Boulevard*
and *Gettysburg Review* in the USA. She lives
in Brooklyn.

A NOTE ON THE TYPE

This book is set using Bembo. The first of the Old Faces is a copy of a roman cut by Francesco Griffo for the Venetian Printer Aldus Manutius. It was first used in Cardinal Bembo's *De Aetna*, 1495, hence the name of the contemporary version. Although a type cut in the fifteenth century for a Venetian printer, it is usually grouped with the Old Faces. Stanley Morison has shown that it was the model followed by Garamond and thus the forerunner of the standard European type of the next two centuries